by Mary Lee Settle

Charley Bland

CHARLEY BLAND

Mary Lee Settle

FARRAR · STRAUS · GIROUX

NEW YORK

We are put on earth a little while
That we may learn to bear the beams of love.

WILLIAM BLAKE

And why beholdest thou the mote that is
in thy brother's eye, but perceivest not the
beam that is in thine own eye?

LUKE 6:41

Contents

What are you going to write about now?

Profane love.

Oh goody! Will there be a killing?

Well, yes and no.

Oh.

Charley Bland

A Triangle of Stone

It seemed that when I was growing up, all the wild roads led to Charley Bland.

Everything brave, vicious, daredevil, lithe was either blamed on him or admired in him, depending on who you were and how old. He made other people feel as if they were plodding. He belonged to everybody and nobody, athlete and comforter, even when he drank, and he drank a lot.

I always, then, glimpsed him turning away, going someplace else. He was, in those days, years older than I was—ten to be exact. But at fourteen, twenty-four exists in an unattainable world. For us, looking on, he acted out our dreams of what we could hope to do when we grew up, if we only had the nerve.

He was a good man, in his own way. Everybody said so. They said he would do anything in the world for you.

Charley Bland

Men loved him and women were in love with him, whether they were children or grownups, and whether they knew it or not. Crazy about him, they said, and they were right. He was the kind of man a woman falls for. Crazy—falling—when we heard that, it opened up possibilities that made us put our heads together and whisper.

Charley and his friends called themselves the sacred circle. They were rumored to do things nobody else dared to do. When I was eight, and Charley eighteen, we saw them one night at Halloween. There were four of us, all best friends. We were dressed in old-fashioned costumes with hoop skirts; we clung together as well as we could with the hoops, and wandered, a clutch of little girls, through the scariest night of the year.

Charley and his friends didn't even know who we were. They had never looked down that far. They ran past us down Beauregard Street. The others were soaping the lozenge-shaped stained-glass doors of the houses that had been built sometime in the nineties and were not places where anybody we knew lived, except girls who went to school in silk dresses.

Then Charley Bland ran down the street behind the others, and broke every door with a baseball bat and was gone before anyone could see him. A man caught me by my hoop skirt and tried to make me tell, but I didn't. Nobody ever told on Charley Bland. The plain glass lozenges exist still as his monument. I remember looking down at the shards of colored glass on the sidewalk, shining red and blue in the streetlamps.

He and Plain George Potter, his best friend, and some of the others, all in their golf shoes and Argyle sweaters like the Prince of Wales, drank bootleg whiskey and held a contest peeing up at the chandelier in the ballroom at Canona Country Club for bets. The rumor was that Kitty Puss Wilson was the judge. As for her, I still hear her laughing at something that I was too young, too far away to hear. They drove fast and lived on tightropes of chance, and only their imitators were killed.

It seemed to me, sitting by the swimming pool when I was fifteen, trying to be longer-legged than I was, that there was brimstone and sunshine when they occupied the pool like invaders. When Charley Bland entered the water, his dive was so clean there was only a parting, not a splash.

Through the years, these glimpses remain with me of Charley Bland, the wild colonial boy from the song we called his theme song. He was graceful when he walked, as men are graceful, contained, easy and quiet, head stooped a little, thoughtful and alone, even in company. I see him still as he was then. Someone calls to him, and, his head half turned, suddenly there is a smile so happy he looks brushed by angels.

He was caught pushing a cart down the main street of Canona, dancing with a lamppost, driving his car slowly along the sidewalk at four o'clock in the morning, following Kitty Puss and Plain George. They were all drunk. He had come home from one of the schools he seemed to pass through like railroad stations. People said that Charley Bland's mother was just worried sick about him, "just" meaning infinite, not "fair" or "only." We lived and spoke in the South.

We shared crushes on Charley Bland as we did on movie stars; he was as far away as that to us. We told each other on long telephone calls that we had seen him, here or there, in odd places, always unexpected. He passed along our lives with the air of a man who has come back from dark streets, not giving a damn. When he was twenty he seemed to us much older; we gave him in our whispers the sophisticated age of twenty-five; later he seemed much younger. There was an evasive adaptability about him, a camouflage.

Sometimes when I see him as he was then, I think of flying, or of diving under the sea, but it is I who have done these things, not Charley Bland. But he is there still, the old illusion of him as he was before I knew him, dancing through my dreams, light, balanced, poised on the edge of secrets.

Then, in one day, he fell. It was the day after the Sunday of Pearl Harbor. Of course he volunteered. But Charley Bland, the shining adolescent, was found to have a flawed heart. I only knew this years later. All I remember of him then was from when I came back after the war. It was a glimpse, as usual, but so different. He was standing in a long greatcoat on a street corner, his face in the repose of habitual longing. For the first and last time that I knew him, he looked old, neglected, dirty. I don't think I had ever seen a man returning from a bender before. I thought then that he had had a hard war.

All Charley Bland had needed was unnamed grief. Women after that were doomed to him.

On the first of April 1960, as I had done every year since the Second World War, which we thought of simply as the war, I came back from France on my yearly duty visit. I meant to stay a month. But Charley Bland saw me, walked into my life and mind, and set a place there he would not leave.

Fifteen years of self-imposed exile that I had thought of as escape became unreal: unreal years, unreal choices, unreal cities. The friends I left, the understanding of what I had been trying to do for so long, the beginning of recognition after years of work, faded into something ephemeral, unconsidered. I had had no idea how fragile it was, or, in that brute and tender capture, that anyone I had left behind cared. In rejecting it all, I did not even give it the honor of disdain.

The circular travel from home to home had begun in 1944, when, after my first year at Nelson-Page, I went to visit my grandmother in Florida. The ladies there entertained English airmen who were in training; the RAF had won the Battle of Britain and was historic and glamorous to them. They saw the weedy eighteen-year-old boys as heirs to Douglas Bader. They commandeered girls to help them make the young strangers feel at home.

One week after I met Wenty Bredon, we ran away and married. He had a three-day pass. We were nineteen. Things like that happened then. We grabbed at life, hungry for it. One late night he had one of those shivers of fear he suffered, as they all did, from time to time, and he said somebody was walking over his grave. He asked me to promise him that if he was shot down I would take his place. Well, Wenty wasn't shot down. Two months later he crashed on a training exercise called circuits and bumps. I still hear the slow march they played on the way to the growing little cemetery near the airfield, and he was buried under a Florida sky. On the way back from his funeral the RAF band played a quick march. After a few years I could no longer recall what Wenty looked like.

I kept my promise anyway. I wangled my way to England and joined the WAAF. In 1946 I went to live in Paris, because I didn't want to leave Europe. At first my father sent me money, because I had been in the war and was a widow and twenty-one years old, but soon the drama of that faded from my parents' minds, and they began to try to lure me "home."

I joined UNESCO. Everybody did except the boys on their GI bills, and they already had money. By 1950, when I had been trying to write for several years in the mornings before work, and in the evenings when I was too tired, I gave up what my parents called a perfectly good job with the government. I kept body and soul together by finding fancy freelance work—covering the Paris fashion openings, writing travel articles, testing restaurants for the growing American peacetime invasion. I did it all, and then disappeared back to Saint-Germain-des-Prés, where my friends were.

I see now that the way we lived was a different kind of American convention. We talked about Kierkegaard and suicide and families. I tried to look like Juliette Greco, or a gamine, depending on the mood and the time of year.

We read each other's short stories and were sure we were better writers than most people who had been published. Some of us saw ourselves as heirs to "Papa" Hemingway and Scott Fitzgerald. Some of us were more erudite than that. We saw ourselves instead as the children of Pound and Eliot and the more evasive French—Alain-Fournier, Radiguet, the romantic surrealists, the young dead. We clung together like the refugees we were, nurtured each other's talent and tentative hopes, scorned popular success, and wrote obsessively about what we had left behind. After ten years I published at last, a short, acerbic novel that I see now could have been written by any one of us who were reading Camus at the time.

For five of those years I had lived with a painter, up five floors in an apartment off the rue Jacob that smelled of cabbage, and where the dim light I punched to see my way up the ancient stairs went out before I got to the next landing and the next button. I opened the door to a clean scent of turpentine and paint I have found comforting ever since. We shared what money we could find, and drank Algerian wine, and were good to each other, and we never quarreled, which I see now was a bad sign. I tried sometimes to ask my family to help me, but they disapproved of everything I was doing, although they didn't quite understand or care what it was.

Once a group of the girls I had grown up with were coming together to Paris. My mother wrote and said that if I would stay with them in their hotel in what she called downtown Paris, and be with my own kind and see things with them, she would send me the money. I made the mistake of saying that I could live for four months on it, so if she would send it I could go with the girls—I made a funny story of it at the café—and show them the sights. She wrote back and said she had found she simply couldn't afford it.

Charley Bland blew away all I had built, quite casually, and gave me in its place a caul of illusion of bright clarity where drabness became subtlety, dust and neglect became old rose and damask, and an ordinary family grew larger somehow than the people I had known and cared for. They were more significant, their power greater, their punishments more painful, their exiles, meted out so casually, a death.

The face of this love was quiet and feral. It was a ruthless act, but not a guilty one. A waterfall, a flood, is neither guilty nor not guilty. It simply drowns the people in its way. I was caught in a storm, a *coup de foudre*, a dream come true in all its terror.

It was, for both of us, a dangerous meeting. Each of us had lived too long in the other's fantasy. My memory of my childhood home had invaded my other life only in banal dreams that I ignored. His dream of "going places and doing things," as he said I had done, made a romance for himself out of the life he thought I lived, out of war and being poor and living in Paris, the city of his dreams.

A safety he didn't have drew me. A glamour I no longer considered drew him. It was inevitable. There was even, God help us, a triangle, as there has to be in orthodox romances. It was the deepest, oldest, most insoluble triangle of all.

I know that the love I lived in then was profane. But it had its stations, its parodic crucifixions, its shallow sacraments.

I have needed an image to exorcise it, why it happened, to blot it out at last if I can, because it is a haunting, this place into which, at any time through all the years since, without warning, I have fallen.

This is the way it begins. I see a woman. The woman is myself, and not myself, as in a dream. It is night.

I am sitting in the front seat of a car that smells of leather and tobacco smoke and rain. The motor idles. Everything is significant, as in madness or drugs, edged with bright definition like those shards of stained glass so long ago. The windshield wipers move back and forth, back and forth, click then click then click then click, a metronome that gives this image rhythm.

But there is no time. Where I am, where the car is, the street, the town, the night, there is no time. It exists in a timeless center, which I do not yet know is a prison.

There is the smell of tobacco, rain, linen, and night. I sit there, my hands in my lap, hypnotized with patience, watching the rain, shunted by the wipers, break and scatter the streetlights. The pavement is sleek with night rain, and makes the city clean when it is not clean, another illusion.

I am not smiling, but I am happy, empty, weightless, floating, willing to wait. I have become, by this unrecognized defeat, a woman in a story, not a love story—but a story to explore love, and so, an adventure.

One night, a night in late April, I sat waiting and watching the rain. By late April it had come to this. A seed fluttered down from a tree along the city street, winged down, fallen in the flowing gutter, and the rain jostled it, swept it along, and it let the water carry it, the winged green seed. I heard the touch of fingers on the closed window and thought at first that it was the wind or the rain, but it was Charley Bland's hand, and he had in it a key.

Homeless for another night, we have found a hotel room, a bar-room joke which I do not know is a joke, and I do not yet know that he has been at home in it many times before and knows how to do this. He has had many homes.

We move toward each other across a worn brown carpet as if we had a long way, running past barriers, great piers, ancient wharfs, barrels tumbled in our paths to keep us apart, the jeers of the dockers, rain, always rain that will later be snow, rain and darkness, and we find each other at last, thirsty and secret.

The room glows, our bodies confess their need for each other. Then, absolved for another night, we lie quiet on the narrow bed, watching and not watching a dim print of the New River Gorge that has brown stains at the corner, and talk. He calls someone an eccentric and I ask him what an eccentric is. Somebody, he says, you ask to dinner once a month and who is not very good in bed. He lights a cigarette.

But we have not come long distances from great wharfs. Like the room, we are a joke. Charley is forty-five years old and I am thirty-five and we have been entangled too long in our youth. I have moved back into my parents' house. He has never left his. The two houses are so close to each other that we both say good night to the lights in each other's window that we watch go out at bedtime. We have told our mothers that we are going to the movies. They both know where we are, but this hotel is a convenience for them and for us. It does not disturb the status quo. We lie and they know it, but we are made vulnerable by love and we are overaware of hurting them.

There are scars on the dresser, which has a tiny television on it that does not work. The light of our love has dimmed and the room is dun-colored again. It is in the corner of the hotel, and we could, if we tried, see across the deep river. I sleep for a second and I am in the river, going deeper and deeper. He wakes me. He is lonely to talk more. He says you can make love to anybody, but he can talk only to me.

He tells the truth always, no matter how harsh, priding

himself on that to hide the essential lie, that his freedom is a quest, not real, a secret that everybody knows. He makes a drink in the thick hotel glass. The room is scented with bourbon. He wraps himself in the bedcover and stalks about the small room, accusing me, telling me that the woods are full of people who are just as intelligent as I am but who don't know how to speak.

"Why, I know men . . ." he says, and stops, not because he is hiding anything, but because he has noticed a light across the river where the hills are and where we have come from. "We have to go," he says. He is even sad about this, but he does nothing about it.

We have existed for a few hours in this rented center. All the glow to sustain us until the next escape will come from here, from the deceptive clarity of this bright prison, this dun-colored room, through the rain, to the tears that will turn to snow.

This hotel has been named for one of the South's first abolitionists, the most famous man from this valley, but everybody here has forgotten him and takes the name for granted.

When I began to dive deep into the ocean, I was within a perfect microcosm, and so I recognized it again, the small round world cut off by stillness. I would sit and wait, thirty meters down, with the same patience demanded by this love, for a spear fisherman I was not strong enough to follow, trusting in return because he has signaled yes. I sat on the sea floor within the circle of my vision in the water world, conscious of bright detail, a frond, a sponge, and I knew that the bright colors were deceptive in the deep prism that surrounded me. The red had turned to green; in the green-blue world green blood flowed. There was a separateness, even of the sand. My slow breathing was at the center of a vast silence, the rhythm of the rising bubbles like the rhythm of the windshield wiper, the dim hotel room, the rain.

Earlier I had played a game, from the time I was a child. It was a game of freedom and survival. I would choose a square, always a square of space, a wasteland, an abandoned yard, the corner of an empty field passed in the car, and given that image, I would dream of survival in my own square space of the world, constructing my life on what it contained, as in the dun-colored hotel room containing love.

So the recall that has begun my quest to find out why all this happened is not of a presence but rather of an absence, and I am under the sea, or waiting in a car in a dark street in the rain, or constructing safety in the square of the hotel room. The car lights and the streetlights shine on the dark wet street, rhythm of the breath bubbles and the wipers, the moan of the engine, waiting in a clear world of water, alone, not with the other, in the safety of his absence when therefore he is perfect, hunter diver, small-town lover. I am waiting, patient, weightless, as later in prayer or work, a sense that I am in the right place at the right time.

The mistakes of the past, holy, deceptive, innocent, and ruthless, guide us to our absolutions.

On the hill across the river, listening through the rain for the same car to turn into the driveway of her house and relieve her of her boredom, a relief she thinks of as love, Mrs. Bland, Charley's mother, the third in the triangle, a small woman with a sweet rosy face, sits playing solitaire, which she carefully calls Canfield. She tends to slap the cards down because there is a residue of fury in her hand she does not recognize, dissatisfactions she does not name, and small dangers that would turn large if she did not manipulate others to protect herself.

Mr. Bland has gone out and so has her sister, Dearie, and she resents being alone for an entire evening. She glances again out of the window and sees the tiny light go off across the river, sighs, and smiles.

There is the power of centuries in her hand, as strong and ruthless and directional as the rain which will not stop, and it annoys her. She does not fear the new woman, someone she has known all the child's life, or thinks she has; she still thinks of her as a child. There have been so many and will be for so long and she is so tired of bothering, but knows she must. She fears that her son has drunk too much and has driven too late up the slick street. An *agacement* she calls prayer takes care of that.

He drives home late. It is home to him, not life. Life is now, in the car. It is his only time alone, away from the women who love him. Under the wet trees the headlights are a bright path between demands he has long since known he cannot meet, except by deceiving them both. He is at peace.

The woman is in the car, waiting.

The man is driving under the trees.

The hand hovers over the ace of diamonds.

Let me explain this triangle. It is the stuff of jokes, and comic strips, and suicides. It is the mother and the son and the woman, whether she is holy, whore, or wife.

Mrs. Bland hears the car engine shut off, and then the door open into her pale-green hall with the roses in her favorite vase, as if she had put them there for welcome. She pretends, flirting a little by habit, that she is too engrossed in her game to notice. His hand touches the red ten and moves it to the black one-eyed jack. He smiles, flirting by depreciating, as Southern men are taught to do, making her feel young and foolish, silly-billy, and lovely, a girl, a "gel," she would say, carefully.

His affection that she expects flows through the gesture, the play she has missed, but what she sees for a second is the hand of a child. She does not look up. She has taken the warmth of his return for granted.

These acts may have happened on different nights in different years, even to different women, for the players have changed many times, while they, the mother and the son, the woman, remain the same for a pause in time.

For me they will stay that way, though they are dead, unresolved, unless, at last, I resolve them. He will remain a forty-five-year-old man, too young for his years, she a woman of seventy-nine, seventy-nine forever in my haunted house.

This is the triangle of stone, more brutal and more ancient than the romantic triangles in love stories. This is the mother, the son/lover, the woman forever watchful, an unholy trinity.

But I have come long ago from a lost place that makes me vulnerable to these deceptions. Like Charley Bland's heart, I have an unknown flaw. The face that he has seen in me is his, unlived; I see in his another face, too, benign, half-forgotten, and powerful.

Bobby Low

Bobby Low let me swim on his back, holding on around his neck, and he said, "Not too tight, you'll choke me."

I smelled tobacco and sweat and hair and creek water, green smell, fish smell, rock smell, smell of afternoon with the sun heating the surface of the water and down below cold when he told me to put my feet down. I drew them up again and wrapped my legs around his body.

The sun cast the shadow of the high cliff across the swimming hole. It made the little ledge below it dark. I was afraid of it, but I didn't tell him. The ledge was five feet above the water and the high cliff was fifteen feet; they were God's stairway. The high cliff's shape, and the pine tree up on top of it, with the green mountain behind it, Big Cumberland, were written with shadow across the water and we swam into it. My brother told me it was bottomless there, all the way to China, and that there was a thing living in a cave under the cliff that would eat my feet.

But on Bobby Low's back I was safe. He could do anything he wanted. He wasn't afraid of anything except, Mamma said, a man's responsibility, not meaning me to hear, or maybe she did; she was always talking about seeing things as they were and a little dose of truth never hurt. But she said that he was as attractive as her daddy, who had been a devil with the women, too.

Once we were driving in the night, following our headlights that swung out over space and then bounced against Cumberland Mountain as the old road climbed around it. We had been to Middlesboro, the center of the world in those days. In the darkness of the car, they were all singing sweet and low, because people sang that way when Bobby Low was around. He knew all the songs—"Little Cory" and "The Wreck of the *Titanic*" and "The Wild Colonial Boy" and "The Wings of an Angel" and "My Name Is Billy" and "Froggie Would A-Wooing Go" and "The Sweetheart of Sigma Chi" and "Yes! We Have No Bo-Nan-Os." I was three-quarters asleep, lying against Genevieve's breast in the front seat between them. She always let me do that. Mamma didn't; her body froze when I touched her there, but she did try to stand it.

Bobby Low saw a pile of logs up ahead across the road and he didn't think, he just swerved around it on the outside where there was a drop of a thousand feet, but he went so fast and gauged it so well that as I woke up I swear we were floating through air, and he landed us in the Packard on the other side of the pile of logs with the hillbillies who were going to rob us just standing there beside it with their faces open in the moonlight and swept behind us staring, and one of the women in the back seat screamed. It was over in about a breath and we went on and Genevieve patted my head and hugged me. She looked calm and her blond hair shone in the car lights like a halo.

The sun was always shining in Genevieve's room in her parents' house. It filtered through the organdy curtains onto her brush-and-comb set, and her nail buffer and her mirror had silver backs that caught the light. Her dressing table was blond, too, blond wood. Mamma said it was French, painted French vanilla, like ice cream. Her bed had a soft pink cover on it with lots of pillows that were as light as air and had ruffles made of white voile with what Mamma said was eyelet embroidery; eyelets, little eyes.

There was a faint mist of powder on the dressing table from the Coty's box, orange with white powder puffs painted on it, that looked as soft as she was. She knew I loved the box, so she gave me one and I took it with me to Florida and it got thrown away. She said try as she might she never could get rid of the faint powder dust, but I liked it. It was like the halo of her blond hair.

I saw her a lot of the time in what she called "dishabille" with a little laugh, like people added when they used old-fashioned words. It was really a Japanese kimono that was different colors in different lights. She would sit at the dressing table in her dishabille, and she would let her hair down. Whenever I heard that saying, "to let your hair down," I always saw her, sitting at her dressing table, smiling into the silver-backed mirror with her curly initials etched on it, that she held in her hand so she could see the back of her head in the dressing-table mirror, letting down her bright hair like Rapunzel. It fell all the way to the floor.

Genevieve and Bobby Low were married, but they

didn't live together except once in a while, first at one parents' house and then at the other's. Genevieve had a disability which I matched with her dishabille. I heard Mamma say they had run off to Maryland, and that Mrs. Grieves never would have sanctioned it had she known before it was too late. My brother told me that meant they stayed all night together in the John Marshall Hotel in Richmond, Virginia. Mamma said Genevieve never complained. Genevieve in dishabille, never complaining; that was what a woman was like, soft and blond.

Sometimes in the afternoons we sat on the porch of Mrs. Grieves's house and watched her colored man cutting the lawn. She never said his name, so I never knew it. He moved back and forth, and the burr of the lawn mower and the smell of the grass was what summer afternoons were, that and grownup voices and snatches of laughter.

The porch went around three sides of the house, so that you could sit in the shade whatever time of day it was, and there were three swings for three times of day, and green-and-white-striped awnings and white wicker chairs and tables, and the women wore gray georgette, at least Mrs. Grieves did, gray georgette with a Val lace collar over a shelf of bosom, and sometimes a voile fichu with little pink roses embroidered on it and a little watch pinned to the front. She wore little glasses that Mamma said were pince-nez, pinch-nose.

She smelled old, combined with Yardley's Lavender or sometimes Roger & Gallet's Violet. Genevieve would trail her hand over the arm of the swing and rock gently with her feet and make the swing creak. They would talk about people, who was fast and who had gone off with somebody and who was coming to visit and who was going to be in the weddings, all in the shade, the summer shade, the green shade with the women waiting in it for evening to come. The breeze made the other swings creak in the distance, and sometimes I could hear the *thunk thunk* of the beaten-biscuit machine on the back porch that meant Mrs. Grieves was going to have a Circle meeting, and no one had lost their money yet.

I sat on the porch floor and let my legs hang down among the cosmos and baby's breath Mrs. Grieves's colored man planted there every year. The floor felt slick. It was painted green every spring. Mamma said that Mrs. Grieves was a meticulous housekeeper.

I didn't listen to the murmured voices of the grownups somewhere above me, but I heard some of it anyway through my own dreaming and hoped that for once nobody would move or change anything. I wanted to feel safe there, but I couldn't because Mr. Grieves owned the bank and had Daddy in the palm of his hand.

Bobby Low's house wasn't on a street with a lawn in the front. It was on a hill, up a steep road, and it had been there a lot longer than Mrs. Grieves's house. Even the porch was different, the dark green of its shade came from the high trees all around it and the smell was of tree sap and dew and dogs. The floorboards hadn't been painted for so long that they had their own color showing again, like the Lord had meant them to be streaked like that, back to nature, Bobby Low said. The swing was in the deepest shade of the porch, and the shade didn't move around. It was there all the time. Little spindled columns held the porch up, and there was wooden lace all around the porch ceiling.

The hall had big stairs and it was dark wood, carved as in a castle. It had dark-red wallpaper that Mrs. Low said had been there since the year dot. Everything else was dark green, as if it had grown on the edge of the woods and the meadow instead of being put there, even the living room where we sat in the wintertime, and the dogs lay all over the Oriental rug that was threadbare and nobody gave a damn. Sometimes Mrs. Low read to me, *Candide* and *Gulliver's Travels*. She said I ought to know them. They were her favorite books. Mrs. Low and Mrs. Grieves didn't speak to each other. Mrs. Grieves blamed Mrs. Low for the marriage. Mr. Low was dead. Sometimes she wound up the Victrola and played Paderewski and Galli-Curci.

Mamma had those records, too, and some others, "The Old Rugged Cross," which my other grandmother, my daddy's mother, gave her for a Christmas present and she had to keep for when she visited, and "All Alone by the Telephone." Our books were not the same, though. Mamma read us *A Child's Garden of Verses* and *Songs of Innocence* and the Waverley Novels, and I read *The Arabian Nights' Entertainments*, which I found in the Harvard Classics for myself when nobody was paying attention. But ours were the only two houses that had any books at all. The rest had magazines.

Bobby Low taught me to scratch the dogs with my foot on the belly and see them smile, Dan and Jubal and Johnny and Lily. Mrs. Low said the house was run for them, but she didn't sound like she cared. She was as small as Mrs. Grieves was large, spindled, like the porch columns.

In the fall Bobby Low would take me to run the dogs before the hunting season opened. I could see it opening, like a door. He said the mountain people made their own hunting season, when they were hungry or when the birds had raised their young. It was a natural time. There had to be some leaves off the trees so he could hear the birds, and see them flying between the bare branches.

He didn't take me when they were hunting, only before, up behind the house on the hill, where the home coveys were, three of them, and the grass of the big meadow was up to my shoulders. He had sown the meadow with what the coveys liked, lespedeza and cinquefoil. At the edge of the meadow he had planted a thorn-apple tree a long time ago, when he was a boy.

I could see the high feathered tails of Dan and Jubal and Johnny and Lily, at the level of my eyes, as they paused and checked back to see where he was. "Look at them damn dogs hightail it through the grass," he said, pleased with them. He talked hillbilly only when he was with me and the dogs. He had been to Princeton, where all the men in the coal business went.

I never heard him raise his voice. He signaled with his arm and with a little whistle. Once, when Lily flushed a bird too soon, he just looked at her and said "Shame," so that only she could hear and not the other dogs, and she turned and flounced back home without another word from him.

He was the same way with me, soft voice saying, "Keep up, you have to keep up if you're going to run the dogs." I would swim through the tall grass, parting it with my body and trying to keep up so I wouldn't be sent back to the house like Lily.

I was in love with both of them, together, as one flesh, as the Bible says, married, when the two are as one. So with Bobby Low letting me swim on his back, and Genevieve on the bank watching us, how could I be scared?

Bobby Low was not Daddy. Daddy sat across the creek, watching us, too. I felt sorry for him. He tried to swim me like Bobby Low did, and I screamed with terror because he had love only in his brain and not in his hands. He couldn't help that. He did try. Mamma said he was worried to death. He thought if he worried about us all, all the time, we would know he loved us. At least that was how Mamma explained it when she said, "Leave your daddy alone. He's worried to death." It was because Genevieve's father held our life in his hands, like holding infinity in the palm of your hand in the *Songs of Innocence*.

Daddy was different from what you meant when you said father, though. One kind of father was like Mr. Grieves, who was without mercy and held your life in his hands. The other kind was more like Who art in Heaven, and looks down, and won't let a sparrow fall, and all that. Bobby Low was more like that kind of father. It wasn't the same.

We swam across the deepest part of the creek, way over my head and even over his, and he turned his head a little, just paddling along so I would, he said, get used to it and never be afraid of the water; that was an order. He couldn't stand that, people who were afraid of things, so I never let him know. He would say, "God, I can't stand that," and turn his back on anything cruel or anything boring.

His eyes were so close to me that I could have licked them, sweet eyes, kind, but I didn't. We went across the creek like two otters, making no waves, just a water path, and people swimming near us looked that way people do who think they ought to with their mouths and faces all sweet, but not their eyes, which are the windows of the soul—he told me that over and over—and are going to forget you the minute you pass. They couldn't fool me. To tell the truth, nobody could. I knew the difference and I knew the signs. He taught me, but I already knew anyway.

He jumped from the ledge with me in his arms, and we flew for a long time in the green air, floated and flew at the same time, and then we passed through the shadow on the water and right under and up again, and he let me hold my nose.

Then he said, holding me close, "Now, you open your eyes under water. It won't hurt you and I want you to see what's down there." So we went under and I opened my eyes, and I saw vague big legs swimming along up above me, dead white legs, and a misty fish came over and nudged us and Bobby Low's eyes laughed. Everything was bigger than above the water.

We came up into a new world for a minute, where the shadows had changed their drawing and the trees towered over us, and Genevieve called from the bank, "You'll drown her." We were on the edge of things, the edge of the water and the edge of the cliff, and the edge of the road like the flying in the night, and so long as he was there nothing could happen, because he had, they said, the timing of a great athlete. He had been a quarterback at Princeton. Mamma said he never got over it, and that was mean, even if it was true. She never did learn that true didn't have to be mean.

He was big and red and brown, but light. He walked on the balls of his feet like an Indian. He didn't give a damn, even when Genevieve's father said, "You could have wrecked my Packard," not considering the fact that there were six human beings in it. As Mamma said to Daddy, "Isn't that just like a banker?"

Uke was courting my aunt. Everybody called him that because he was learning the ukulele with a flashlight under the covers at the clubhouse at No. 10 mine. He was standing up there on top of the highest rock. He stood in the last of the sun and he should have looked like an angel but he didn't. He looked cold and his legs were skinny, and he was obviously waiting for my aunt to look at him. When she did he jumped from the high rock, but she had already turned around talking to somebody and didn't even look. Bobby Low said so that nobody but me could hear him, "Oh my God, honey, see me, Mabel!" That meant show-off. "If you want to do something like that, Little Onion"—he called me that—"and God knows we all do, do it for yourself to see if you can." He meant not to say "See me, Mabel."

Then he hugged me and told me that one day I would swim the Cumberland River, not this little old creek. "One of these days," he said, like the song. So I promised myself I would swim the river, and I would do it by myself to see if I could, and not say "See me, Mabel."

He said that the water that was holding us up and all around us was a source. He said he had seen it, away up the creek where it ran right out of a hole in the world, that's the way he said it, a hole in the world, and it ran down through rills and hills and bushes and branches. He made it sound like a song, too, so I would never forget it, where the source of the Atlantic Ocean was. We were floating in it, right there.

"Just like the veins and the arteries and the nerves that run through you," he said in my ear, "where the legs join the body join the neck join the head join the brain join the soul." He explained that it was the same way with the little creek, Bloody Run because a man was found in it face down, dead and scalped; Bloody Run ran all the way to the Cumberland River, which ran all the way to the Mississippi, which ran all the way to the Gulf of Mexico, which ran all the way to the Atlantic Ocean, and I could see the man's blood running all the way to England in the Gulf Stream, which Bobby Low said was a river in the ocean.

Genevieve called from the bank, "Come out. It's time for the picnic," and we got out when she said to, both of us, standing there with the creek weeds and the creek water flowing down our bodies, and we looked, she said, like something drownded. "Undine," she said, and kept her hand on my wet head until I could feel the warmth she was sending me. Mamma called out, "Wrap a towel around yourself before you turn blue."

So we walked all the way back down to the ford, and we crossed the creek where it was shallow, and went to our own picnic ground. It was a little glade right in the middle of the woods that Bobby Low had found when he and Bobo Jenkins went hunting. Mamma said he didn't have an ounce of discretion about his friends.

There was the place where they had made the fire the year before, where they had banked rocks around in a circle. Everybody moved around doing things. Mamma set up a card table, and one of the men said, "You don't want a table for a picnic."

She said, "I do. I can't stand dirt. Put that in your pipe and smoke it." She had started saying that a lot, like a habit, and I did, too. "I'm not scared. Put that in your pipe and smoke it," I said to my brother when he told me a blue light would come down over the city, when we didn't even live in a city. We lived in a town, Pineville, Bell County, Kentucky, the dark and bloody ground. He told me Ichabod Crane and the headless horseman were coming right down Pineville Street in the night to get me. "Put that in your pipe and smoke it."

We all went into the woods and picked up pieces of wood and piled them in the middle of the stones. Some of the men said, "Not that way, this way." They argued and pushed and pulled at the wood until it was a big pile that did to suit them. Then they lit the fire and we watched it lick up, blue at the beginning and then turning red and yellow, and crackling at the branches we gathered as if it were trying to break them. The fire settled to blue in the last daylight, and the smell of potato salad and fried chicken and baked beans and watermelon and pickles and coffee and angel-food cake, all together with the smell of the fire and the blue flames, meant that it was a picnic.

Bobby Low buried potatoes in the embers the minute the fire banked down enough. I went to the bathroom in the same place I had the year before. There was a snake, but I just got the hell out and didn't say anything, because I was afraid the women would all pack up the picnic and go home.

It was the most important picnic of my life, because my brother had told me it was going to be the last one so I might as well enjoy it. He was better at overhearing what Mamma and Daddy were talking about than I was. He told me that Mr. Grieves had foreclosed and had said, "Well, what can I do?"

I could see Mr. Grieves just closing his hand and all of us caught inside. My brother told me it was because the bottom had dropped out of the coal business. I knew it was true, because Mamma read late the night before the picnic and fanned around the dark house in her nightgown. I could hear her, walking back and forth, onto the living-room rug and off again. When she finally came to bed she got in so that Daddy wouldn't wake up, but later I heard her sobbing, trying not to make any noise. The little sound reminded me of Bobby Low's song about the lonesome train whistle.

At the picnic she had dark circles under her eyes and she didn't sing when the others did.

Dark doesn't come down. You don't notice, you just watch the firelight getting brighter and brighter, and then it is night. I lay in Bobby Low's lap, nearly asleep, and the fire sang and breathed and I could feel him breathe, too. He pointed up at the black mountainside and said, "See the stars." There were stars spattered all over the side of the mountain, fallen there in the dark. "No," he said, "I was fooling. Those are all the animals that live in the woods and they are watching the picnic. That's the firelight reflected in their eyes."

But it looked to me like a lot of twin stars had fallen over the mountain.

I must have slept, because a woman's scream woke me up, but Bobby Low said it was only a painter on the mountain that sounded like a woman. That's what he called a mountain lion—a painter.

The next thing I knew, I was in the back seat of the car, bumping along the old Bloody Run road, slow because Daddy didn't want to hurt the Chandler sedan. I could see Bobby Low's Stutz Bearcat disappearing down the road ahead of us. My brother was looking out the window, so I couldn't see his face. Mamma glanced back and said, "It's all right. They're asleep," so my brother must have closed his eyes, and I closed mine so she wouldn't see that I was awake, because she wouldn't ever say anything then. Her eyes in the car lights were lit like the wild-animal eyes on the mountain.

I prayed, "Please God please God please God," but it

didn't do any good. We left our house after the books were packed and the furniture. Mamma let me bring one book. I brought two, *At the Back of the North Wind* and *The Arabian Nights' Entertainments*. Nobody was paying any attention to me, so I could do what I wanted, even cry, but I was too dry to cry.

My brother tried to run away, but they found him. Mamma said, "The fathers have eaten sour grapes and the children's teeth are set on edge."

The Chandler was piled high to go over the mountains. Genevieve wasn't there to say goodbye. I heard Mamma say she felt so awful she'd had an attack. But it wasn't her fault.

Bobby Low was there, though, and I can still feel his hug and hear him say, "You'll be back before you know it."

I never saw them again. I kept them in my heart, in my heart of hearts, what a man was, what a woman was.

We drove away, into the cold world. I could see us, with all the other cars and all the other people who had been driven out because the bottom had dropped out of the coal business all over the mountains, in the dark and bloody land, pulling up stakes, which Daddy said meant moving and giving up your claim.

The Rites of Spring

Until my mother met Charley Bland in the parking lot, I kept on going. My family came home to the valley they had all been born in, but in the years by the swimming pool, where Mr. Grieves could never hold us in the palm of his hand again, and Daddy got older and we had money, I was either planning to wander or wandering, looking, I thought, for something up the road, on the train, or down the river, a female Huck Finn in a bathing suit. Then in the parking lot among the Buicks and the Oldsmobiles and the one Bentley in a one-Bentley town, my mother met Charley Bland on the first real spring day.

I am a Southerner, and there is bred in us, as carefully as if we were prize hounds, a sense of betrayal in leaving our roots. We sit in cafés in Paris and pubs in London, everywhere we have landed, and tell stories that sustain us about funny uncles and people up hollows or in small towns with chinaberry trees. So I had come that year in April, as I did every year, to make my apologies for having left home, and my mother had called up to my window in the morning, happy that the early tulips were already in bloom, she said, for me.

The parking-lot attendant knew everybody and had for years. If you had paused that morning, looking for a space where the nice people parked, he would have shaken his head if he didn't know you. You would have seen two people passing the time of day. This is what you see when people meet to plan murder, flirt, or say good morning.

Charley Bland wore one of those hats men wore then, at a Gary Cooper rake, because he had been told he looked like Gary Cooper. He would not have remembered being told that. My mother, some twenty years older, wore, as she always did when she went "downtown," a Davidow suit, of acceptable plaid camouflage.

Her hand was reflected in the rear fender of the Buick. She trailed it delicately as she had been taught to do when she spoke to men, always had done it that way, the way you do it. That hand held ribbons stretching to the past, to where men were, the right kind of men, all the men who made up her approval of Charley Bland.

She had known him for years, and had taken his existence and what we used to call his "bad rep" for granted. But that morning, radiating through and around him, the image of her father was what she said she saw, as clearly as I see you, she said, or the image of someone who might have been her father had he lived. She had seen him last when she was twelve and he died, and after that she had had to construct him, as we would construct God if He did not exist.

"Had my father lived," she would say, imagining another life she never defined.

She saw her father as a rake and a devil, too, unbearably handsome. She had always bought things that he might have liked, a gold watch chain which she wore around her neck over her fawn silk blouse, a fob to match it, an old gold watch. All this had taken years, the old ties she picked up and had made into quilted pillows, "his kind" of chair, the glasses he had taught her were the only kind a gentleman drank from. So many decisions went through the crucible of what the father within her would have chosen that gradually she had dressed her heart's image, constructed from it an inheritance: the watch chain, in her mind, became his; the fob, the old ties, the glasses, all "your grandfather's."

She wanted me home, meaning, of course, her home. There, in front of her in the parking lot, she saw a way. She could never have admitted, even to herself, that she wanted me to be seduced into staying. She only, as she said, wanted what was best for me. There he was, and had been all the time, Charley Bland—as young, to her, as beautiful and devilish as only a mother, a Southern mother, could wish for in a son, and that one thing, what they called the shame about the war, to give him the wound that made him irresistible.

She watched her hand reflected in the car fender, her little hand beginning to freckle, but she was seeing, suddenly, like an inspiration, a plan for me. She was worried about me, she kept saying, I hadn't done anything with my life that was understandable in the terms she, my father, and her father within lived by. She was watching her hand and planning a daughter, as she had for years, entirely innocent of harm and therefore the most dangerous of women.

The hand reflected in the shining fender didn't grasp. She was too certain of what she had in mind for that, and relieved, too. She saw in Charley Bland almost an act of God, turning up like that, she said, as if the thought were inspired.

At first, she told me, he didn't know whether he could or not. I could see him with her, as evasive as a shadow on a wall, until he was certain of what she really wanted. She hadn't needed to say it, spell it out. From old practice he read women. He had always known what promises to make. It was a talent with him.

All she had asked him aloud to do was to take me to a country-club dance, as if I were seventeen and visiting from "out of town." She said that she was so excited when he said yes that she almost ran all the way to Dangerfield's, where the "good" clothes with designer labels came from, and bought me, then and there, she said, a dress to wear.

When she came home I was reading Thomas Hardy and Hardy's Miss Everdene and the dress she lay on the bed like an offering were too volatile a mixture for me to laugh at what she wanted me to do. Besides, it was why I was there, for that deep placation I had carried all my life to make her notice me.

She laid it carefully on the tufted bedspread of the tester bed, with its starched ruffles like an offering, which I thought it was, a pale-fawn handkerchief-linen dress, short and flared at the skirt, shoes for a spring evening, nylon stockings as frail as mist, underwear with lace, as if she were dressing a bride. I found myself loving it. A neglected self within me was almost crying, feeling the fine linen under my hands. It had been a long time, and dedicated poverty had worn me thin.

I loved being dressed in that pale linen, the feel of it after so long against my palms, the touch on my body of delicate underwear and sheer stockings, the shoes with high heels. She had even remembered the scent I had worn when I was growing up and dances were important. If something within me was laughing at all of this, I did not hear it. I was performing a long-forgotten ritual, the ritual of dressing, slowly.

When Charley Bland came to call for me in his white summer dinner jacket, with his smell of clean shaving, his clean linen, and a tinge of bourbon, my father stood in the doorway, smiling. He watched us go up the stone walk past the pachysandra and the mountain laurel he had dug up so carefully in the woods and planted, until we were out of sight around the curve of the path. He had always liked the Blands, he said, and told again about the Bland girls in their white dresses when he was young. I heard the door close softly.

I let Charley Bland place me in the car as if I were a cripple. All the way up the opposite hill, we said little. I see now that there was already nothing we could say.

It is when the ordinary becomes luminous that we are transformed. It is, after all, what fairy tales are about—transformations.

I had gone this way a thousand times, and yet it was the first. We drove down the hill and across the river and past the sidewalk where I had once seen Charley Bland at the end of the war, along the street where the Wayfaring Stranger leaned toward the river, where I had watched him and all the other older ones so often.

It had begun to rain. The street glistened. It was a small

spring rain and then it stopped, and as we began to climb the opposite hill, there was only the scent of it left and the caress of dampness, and the faint smell of tobacco smoke and linen in the dark car.

For the first time since I was six, there was such a total illusion of safety that I nearly slept. I was entranced by it. I was familiar with that safety, as if it were a sixth sense, but it had been dead in me for so long—honed down by war and dedication and being a stranger among strangers to me for so long, constant change and lack of money—that I felt it as new.

Controlled pitch, alert and relaxed was the way he drove, hands easy on the wheel. He glanced at me once, and then watched the road that wound in front of us up the hill, the car lights swinging toward the mountainside, and then the space of the steep slope where in the daylight we would have seen the golf course far below. I had never seen the colors the lights touched so bright—separate leaves, separate branches, a gulf of space, and then a piercing green tunnel of trees where the road from the rain was still so wet it seemed to be made of black water.

We rounded the great curve to the country club, the place where we had all grown up, where all our ceremonies of innocence had happened, weddings, betrayals, seductions, gossip, holidays, parties, all there under the wide trees, and up the grand staircase of what had once been Mr. Slingsby's mansion.

It was the last dance in the old country club before its final move across the river and away from the coal dust and the smell of burning slag that had been creeping nearer and nearer the mansion, as if to remind us of the coal face where it all came from. It was a farewell to childhood and growing up and the time when all troubles were personal, and most of them were secret. I was driving closer and closer to the girl I had left there.

In the awning of light from the porch, he let me out and went to park the car, and I had a moment of fear, fear of the place that I had known so well and rejected so finally, that if I went inside the door, it would close behind me and lock, as if all the life in between had been unreal among unusual people.

To the right of the mansion the pool lay quiet under its floodlights. Light filtered through the vines at the end of the porch and made lace shadows on the stone floor. Up a slope on the other side, the tennis courts were lit, too, lighting the night sky for the party.

I didn't think or consider, I simply felt in my body the need to run away, as I always had, from that dangerous place. But before I could move, Charley Bland was back, and up the steps, and he led me into the huge familiar hall, where the grand staircase wound up and out of sight toward the ballroom, and I can still feel his hand, gentle on my arm.

I had entered a place of ghosts, ghosts climbing the stairs, ghosts calling to each other, ghost laughter, ghosts greeting us, as if I were living one of the dreams I had carried with me for so long.

I had forgotten how clean they all were, how cool and drenched the air of an American country-club dance, where everyone had showered or soaked in scented baths and wore clean clothes that shimmered and whispered of linen and summer voile when the women moved. I heard the whisper of a starched shirt as a man I didn't remember turned his head and called across the hall.

Kitty Puss Baseheart, who had been Kitty Puss Wilson—
I quickly, trained for that, remembered whom she had married—strode across the wide carpet, already half drunk in
dotted Swiss that cost a mint, and slapped me on the shoulder and said, "Jesus, why have you cut off all that beautiful
hair? You look like a convict." She looked from me to Charley Bland and back to me, grinned, and said, "Oh-oh!" and
disappeared before I could say a word.

She hadn't seen me for nearly fifteen years, but it was
her way of greeting me, as if I had gone across the street,
cut off my hair, come back, and become again the child she
half remembered. No time passed with them. I was there.
I was not there. I was there again, taken for granted.

What I was seeing, and not knowing it, was a door of
approval opening at last, longed for without knowing, feared
without facing; I, a runaway, played prodigal, called back.

Plain George hugged me and said, "My God, honey,
how long has it been?" He was wearing a new pink linen
dinner jacket. He said, before Charley could say anything,
"Don't say it. Anne Randolph made me wear it."

The names, the faces were surrounding me, rank on
rank of them, and I had to tell them apart. It was suddenly
easy. They were right. No time had passed. They had weath-
ered a little, but not much. There they sat, the triumvirate,
the fearsome "older girls" of my growing up—Daisy, who
had been at the school I had run away from to go to war,
had chintz roses and lilacs stretched tight across her mus-
cular shoulders. Maria, who had been her shadow at Nelson-
Page, and still was, sat beside her, dressed in a little white
piqué, so like what she had worn for years it seemed a
uniform. Anne Randolph floated at the end of the table in
green chiffon. All their faces were lit by candlelight, and the

kind of welcome travelers have always received, a welcome
left over from when they brought news to farms thirty miles
apart. They had all forgotten, and I, cursed with remembering, was, at least for that night, no man's enemy, forgiving
all in fawn linen.

Anne Randolph made me sit by her. I liked her warmth
and her scent and her dress. She said it was just a little old
thing she'd picked up at Bergdorf, and Plain George, hearing
her, added with that residue of pride that I remembered he
had always had in her, "She still sees every show in New
York." He turned away too quickly to hear her complain,
"Don't say *still*, George, it makes me sound *old*," as if that
thought were the silliest thing she could think of.

But Plain George had already followed Charley to the
long bar at the open end of the grill room. They had, of
course, scorned sitting at the tiny tables at the end of the
ballroom where lesser couples sat, not knowing any better,
in the way of the dancers.

The glasses on the table glittered from the light of the
terrace outside, where it was still too cold to sit, they said.
They seemed still, as they always had, to move in a formal
pattern by the time of the year, to dress by some interior
clock, where in one night all the black dinner jackets disappeared and the white ones, and now the pink, came out
as part of the rites of spring.

There was the sound of ice, the scent of clean shirts
and money and of the spring night around us. Charley Bland
and I watched each other across the room as if we were
alone. The din seemed distant, and we, within it, tried not
to look at each other when we caught ourselves staring.
Charley came over and lifted me up from the table. He said
there was someone at the bar he wanted me to meet. Daisy,

looking after us, sounded disappointed when she said, "I'd like to know who," as if they already knew everybody in the world.

There was talk at the bar in men's voices, lower than the voices of women, more peaceful. They were the men I had known all my first life, who were trained to look after women like me, at least as I was then, in the disguise of the night. The sound of the orchestra was like a whisper away in the distance.

Someone was calling something. I still hear a voice out in the dark, and someone laughing, and a remark from the bar that someone was getting laid on the practice green, how early in the year it was for that, the grass was still wet; seduction, too, ruled by the time of the year.

Charley watched me as if he was trying to understand something he could not name. I watched, too, and waited at a country-club bar where everybody was clean and there were no Jews and there were new pink linen jackets all around me like a barrier against the harsh world and the slag heaps. The self I had pretended for so long did not exist, whom I remembered, if at all, as a girl who had been too aware for where and when she had grown up or not grown up, it seemed, had not been outgrown or defeated. She had simply been left behind to wait for me at a country-club bar where no Jews were let in, still wanting to be like everyone else, still making a hero of Charley Bland, the wild colonial boy, who had turned and noticed her at last.

And there was the door, and it seemed to be opening, and I, as forgiven as the prodigal, walked into that strange perversion that only opened into the past, rejected the present, and ignored the future.

Charley Bland said, "Let's dance," and I knew he didn't

want to, but I followed him up to the great hall and slowly up the grand staircase and into the ballroom. Charley Bland gathered me to him, and seemed to be struck totally still. He said, "Jesus, what's happening to us," and when I started to speak he must have felt the slight pause in my body. He said, "Shut up."

We danced once past the closet door that my best friend and I had found when we were fourteen and had hidden there to watch the grownup dancers, who had seemed then to whirl past our eyes, as light as air, all dancing like Fred Astaire, through the inch-wide crack in the door where we took turns staring.

Charley whispered, "Let's get out of here." That sudden twitch of impatience, the longing to move, was the first of so many times when I sensed a break toward the only freedom he had ever allowed himself flow through his muscles, which were already as familiar as my own.

We didn't go back to the table where the others waited in the shadows for the brightness of the evening to be shed on them by Charley Bland and the newest summer visitor, this one so familiar for so long that nobody had to think of what to say. He almost didn't bother to tell me where we were going, and I was still too shy of him to ask.

"I told Sadie and Cuddy I'd let their dog out. They're in Aiken," he said, and for a minute I thought he was making some sort of joke, and then I remembered them. They were always the other couple at the party, in the car, witnesses to celebration and disaster. I had seen them in Virginia years before at the corner of fields, watching polo matches, horse shows, people they didn't know very well. I had always thought of them, in that long-lost setting, as poor Cuddy and Sadie, and had wanted to protect them. They had seemed old to me then, so vulnerable, standing there on the edge of things.

Charley drove down along the river road and up the hill toward home. It was inevitable that they would live somewhere on that sacred mound. Sadie and Cuddy, named Partlow for his father—I had forgotten that they had been put together in the parceling out of formal marriages. Partlow Bland was the older brother, who some of our parents said was the responsible one. I, who hadn't thought of him for so long, thought suddenly of the older brother of the prodigal. I saw then the prodigal not as myself but as Charley Bland. In all the time or timeless space we lived in together we changed places like that, becoming each other, changing back, reflecting each other like Narcissus and the still water that ran so deep.

Sadie I hadn't known well. She was named Sarah. She was an athletic girl from Kentucky, near Lexington, she had always told us, conjuring bluegrass acres out of the word "near." I remembered her as one of those girls who went in for a gallant ugliness; the name she insisted on using was part of that. It had made her a kind of dictator among the innocent women of what she called her "age group." She set herself to teach them the subtleties of "who you were" fashion. She was an imitator herself of the devil-may-care women she let herself admire, who wore their husband's shirts, beat-up jeans, dung boots, "Wellies." She referred to them all as "the mink-and-manure set." She was as sincere about her horse worship as Attila the Hun.

I remembered her as larger than I was, taking up more space. She was what people called good-looking, as opposed to pretty, when they had to say something about her looks. People said she led Cuddy Bland around by the nose, but the phrase was wrong for him. He was no bull. He was, like many Southern men, saddled with a nickname left over from his childhood. I had always heard that it was because when he was a baby he used to lift his little arms to his mother and ask her to cuddle him. "Cuddy," he said, and he was still lifting his arms, still asking, still being half ignored. My mother said that Charley took up all the family time.

Charley turned the car into the dark road that ran to a small glen at the lower corner of his parents' land, which loomed above us at the crest of the hill. Across a little creek, on the other hill, a light still burned for me in my mother and father's house. I thought, My God, he knows everything. It was the path, now a paved road, to my own secret place when I was growing up. I had found it when my father took the Rabelais I had brought home and threw it out because he didn't want books like that in the house.

It was a frail deserted barn deep in the forgotten grass of a little meadow. It had grown delicate with weather and wind and age, so that it sagged a little, and the bottoms of the upright boards that made its walls were snaggled, and the sunlight and the birds, and once a snake, came in through the wide gaps between them. There was a pile of hay, long left there, that was dry enough to lie on, and I used to sneak down to the little barn and take whatever I was reading, *War and Peace, Anna Karenina, The Picture of Dorian Gray, My Antonia*, all from the library. I never knew which one my father would take away from me.

There I was safe, and read in the sunshafts, and would put the book down and lie there staring at the stains and whorls on the raw board walls until the stains and whorls became old men, watching me. The back of the barn was flush against the edge of the cliff that dropped almost down to the river, and sometimes I would watch the coal barges pass and count them.

Sadie and Cuddy had transformed the barn into a house. I thought at first they had simply torn it down. I could see by the light of the carriage lamp beside the short walk that where meadow grass had been there was a carefully mown lawn; a few of the trees had been left and groomed, so that instead of the straggling branches I remembered, they spread, tamed and shaped, across the grass. Even in the planting near the house Sadie's cult of genteel ugliness had made her choose ugly stalwart plants, prickly holly, mean dark spiky fir.

The whole front was glass. Inside, tangled green philodendron, ivy, and *Monstera deliciosa* made lazy patterns across it. Sadie went in for fleshy leaves. Through their shadows I could see one faint light, and a cavern of a room, four times bigger than my secret horse barn. Except for a few yards of lawn in the front, the house had taken almost all of my meadow.

Charley let me in and went beside the house to let Sadie's dog out of his kennel. It had begun to bark when it heard the car.

Sadie had gone in for textures, too. I sat on the long sofa covered with fawn-colored nubbly cotton that stuck me through my linen dress, and counted fourteen of them while waiting for Charley to return while the dog waited at the kitchen door, refusing, as he said, to do anything but wag its tail and bark.

The floor was terra-cotta tile. The fireplace was a monument of rough stone that rose to a ceiling fifteen feet high. It slanted away from the fireplace down to the only part of my barn that had been left, as for centuries the old has been incorporated into the new. It was the wall of my old men, and there they were still, a little fainter under the "refinishing," polished and burnished and darkened. The slits where the sun had come in had been filled with white plaster, and here and there I could see the faint hint of a brick wall backing them. They were like a mural of my growing up. Years later, in Umbria, I saw paintings on wood of brown saints that looked like my old men, but they had been painted by monks and not the weather.

The lamp I had seen through the glass was a huge green carboy. There had been a murder in London where the killer had dissolved the bodies in acid, brought to his workroom in carboys like that. Its shade was parchment, with holes in it that made a light pattern around the room like one of those glittering balls that used to be in ballrooms. Some of the pillows on the sofa were leather. Some were suede. The rugs thrown over the tiles were Navaho, the fire basket was iron, the fireplace guard copper, the wall behind the fireplace brick, the bar against the fourth wall, where through a door to the kitchen I could hear Charley cursing the dog, was made of wood as gnarled as the old men. Above it a large picture window looked down on the river. It was a room of green leaves, earth colors, and feelies.

Sadie, in her usual fashion, had made a completely modern house, as orthodox as a California dentist's office, but it was the first one on the hill, and she bore out her reputation for being avant garde—a forlorn hope of a woman. She had placed it bravely where all the houses, or most of them since 1936, had been inspired by Williamsburg, so that Queen Anne had entered the hills in a way her troops had never done in her eighteenth-century lifetime. Sadie's was a statement of pastlessness, except for the old men, the watchers from the barn wall, left there for texture and, I thought, for me. I liked it, and I liked Sadie for doing it. The place reminded me suddenly of Girl Scout camp.

Charley came in with a large black retriever lolloping in front of him, making another texture in the big room. The dog jumped on the sofa and began to lick me. I drew back my skirt. I found that I had spread it slightly, so it would look pretty. I was amused at that, at myself petting the dog, at the room, and at Charley pacing up and down across the Navaho rugs, cursing the dog still as a damned bench-bred nuisance not worth fifty cents, and Sadie for not buying a field-bred setter like he had told her to.

He went to the bar and made us drinks. He didn't ask what I drank. He said, "You either drink bourbon or you've quit drinking." Even a choice of alcohol was proof of where you stood and what you thought.

He handed me my drink, and he stood over me, looking down at me, and the first words of love he said were "Why the hell *did* you cut your hair?"

But he touched my head as tenderly as if the cropped hair were a wound. I put my own hand up to stop him, and touched his. That was all. He walked over and sat down in one of the leather chairs, and then he got up and started pacing the floor again, measured and preoccupied. Somewhere in the distance a clock struck twelve. We both counted the slow strikes, and I wondered where Sadie would have allowed the kind of clock that struck like that.

I don't think either one of us drank at all, but the ice

in the glasses in our hands shook with tiny chimes. The minutes tolled and we lived in each other's presence, for a little while totally at peace, as if we had been that way for years and would be for safe undemanding years more.

Charley was the one who said it first and said it then: "Being with you is like being alone," and he looked at the fragments of light through his glass. "Color of a copper penny," he said.

Which of us started to tell all of it, all of it up to that moment as if we had come from a long way away and had to explain the road, how we got there, why we had stayed away from each other for so long, so much wasted time, or then it seemed to be wasted, littered with people who loved us and could hold us away from each other? All this we told each other we knew for a fact, long before he touched me again.

That's when I learned about the war and how it had been for him, a pivot point of his life that held him still. "I tried everything," he said, "even the Red Cross, like a woman," he said with deep contempt, and I knew that he hated and used women and that all I had heard was true, but true for a different reason: he had been acquiescent, not a scavenger.

"That's the one thing I envy in you, that you have been to war." Not that I was a woman, but that closed door was what had made him look at me as if I knew secrets I refused to tell.

I wanted to say something to help, to fit. I couldn't. In that dim room, on that Saturday night, there was no time for easy words anymore. It was already too late to do anything but tell the truth. Raw truth is vulnerable. Judicious truth is the most seductive thing there is. I didn't know that then and I hardly know it now. Even when I see it, I tend to deny that it exists. It seems so unfair.

"It changed me for good," I told him. "I see too much, and things that used to matter don't matter anymore," and then I stopped, because that night they did matter when I had thought all that was over. I was conscious of my judicious clothes and how much the room cost, and how much the life I had chosen to live had cost.

"I don't know," he told the reflection of light through the copper-penny-colored drink. "Something went out of me then. What does the Bible say? Virtue went out of me. There was nothing I wanted to do"—he grinned at me— "except go hunting and court women. My father always said . . ." He retired into the protections of family stories that even Southerners who have not left home tend to use like homesick exiles when the world has grown too harsh for them. "My father," he said again, because the thought of his father had made him pause, "said I never married because I found it more fun to court.

"When you go back"—both of us knowing already I wasn't going back—"I want you to do something for me. I've longed to know the words to a song." "Longed," a favorite word that when used for humans could change lives and not, since it was said casually but not heard that way— a mistake that (let's face it) can sink ships—a word said easily, with all the insouciance and all the charm we've been trained to wish for.

Charley Bland sang the first lines, and I knew he had done that before: "He was a wild colonial boy. Jim Duggan was his name. He came from dear old Ireland, from a town called Castlemaine . . ." He said he had forgotten the rest and he knew I would find it for him and complete it, that most seductive of promises, bring it back from that magic world where the war was and more happened than happened to him and there were such things to be found.

"I could never be a snob again," I told him, as if he hadn't said anything, "and surviving the war, for all of us"—now I was an army, not a woman in fawn linen in a strange familiar room—"was such a miracle that we could take nothing for granted ever again. Not this room. Not these clothes. Not this city. We had seen too much disappear, a house, a friend, in a second, random . . ."

That word stayed in the air with the chiming of the ice in the glasses. I still don't remember that either of us drank.

The clock struck three. The ice was long gone from the glasses. I don't know what had happened to the time. Neither of us had moved. The dog was asleep on another of the leather chairs. As it struck I was still telling him, an Ancient Mariner: "Then it became a kind of holy poverty we all, all of us, everybody who has decided, been chosen, oh, I don't know, to try to write or paint or tell the truth some other way, give up, turn aside from rewards, because we know they aren't there."

I, too, was capable of a story to protect myself. "I remember the day it happened—the decision. I stayed in England because I couldn't stand this country after the war. It was too fat, too healthy, and I was exhausted and I wanted to be where everyone else was exhausted, but I was still tied to all of our past, even after I got back. I was in a hired car going to a wedding at St. Margaret's, Westminster, the daughter of a duchess." He was quiet, waiting. This was the England he knew, duchesses and royalty and castles.

"But at the same time I had been asked to go to a

concert at Wigmore Hall, where there was chamber music. I was wearing a big black hat, and my uniform of consent, a suit by Bianca Mosca, and living on Daddy's money." I rushed on, knowing that these references meant nothing to him, but they were what had been on my road to that room, to Charley Bland. "A Duc de Verdura jewel, and white gloves, always white gloves, and on the way to the wedding I reached out with one of those white paws and knocked on the glass and said, Take me to Wigmore Hall instead, and after the concert a poet I knew and a man who is now one of England's most famous composers and I were walking down Wigmore Street to the Glory Hole, which was terrible but what they could afford, and the poet was wearing my hat and the composer had my white gloves on his ears and we were happy, and on Monday I decided to live in Paris and write fiction and pick up a living where I could, and I always knew I had done the right thing."

I had stood up. "So I cut my hair when I am working so it won't bother me and I become a tonsured monk, if you like, and my life is happy there and I have friends who care for what I'm trying to do and I don't have a cent and it's hard as hell and the man I live with and I have been celibate and faithful for a long time and we've spent only two months of this year together and I'm lonesome as hell, and you can't destroy it because it's all I have, and for God's sake, leave me alone." I was sobbing and so was he. He was holding me and letting old tears fall, and it wasn't the first time I had cried in front of the old men.

"My God, honey, you've been reviewed in *The New York Times*. We all thought you were rolling," I heard him say into my hair, and that was so ridiculous that I laughed while I was crying against the clean linen, and the smell of creek water and sun.

"Doesn't your father send you money anymore?" from somewhere above me. There was no way to answer. It was another language in the world I had lived in where no daddy dreamed of sending money to a thirty-five-year-old daughter who had hightailed it off to God knows where and left a perfectly good job. I didn't want to move away from the safe and lovely shirt. "Goddamn"—voice in the distance. "I wouldn't live that way for ten thousand dollars."

He started to put me down on the sofa as tenderly as he could, but the dog had moved over as soon as I got up and taken up most of it, so he had to move it by its collar, and we fell together on the nubbly cotton, full of laughter, as joyful as children who have come in from somewhere else and are so glad to be there at last that it all seems a blessing, like coming in out of the rain.

The act itself was as gentle and as quiet as drifting off to sleep, the giving in by both of us, me more conscious that it was giving in than he was, and therefore more responsible. But for him, though he stumbled into it, as much a surrender to what he had lost or never found or heard in fragments like the song he sought or feared.

So for Charley Bland it had started as another Saturday night, and he had meant it to be like the others. Visitors, especially summer visitors, had always been fair game, a little something to remember of a visit, not to be taken seriously, never that, some affection and attention, which is what he thought seduction was. The words were all the same. The favorite song was a litany he had used a thousand times before. It always worked, like his friend who always offered a bag of candy; that never failed either.

He said later, and I am sure he believed it, that in the destruction of my carefully built life he was doing me a favor. He hadn't the least idea, to use a phrase current there and then, that he was living a life I would not have chosen for ten thousand dollars. But he had made the past shine; what he promised without saying a word was neither of our real lives but some mutual hope. The part of me I had not let live was no longer rejected. That wandering part of him that had always been secret, because it did not fit the pattern he was asked to cut his jib by, had a hope at last of acceptance, and—here was the miracle for both us—by someone he had known all his life.

On Sunday morning, in the breakfast room that overlooked our garden, where I could see Charley Bland's parents' house, my father looked up over the Sunday paper and smiled with a complicity and approval I had sought all my life, and saw in his face for the first time since I had grown up and gone away and tried to "make something of myself," as he would have said. But what I had made did not exist as a possibility in the horizons he saw; there was too much breakage, of rules, of protections, of lies, and he had hated it all. When I sent the first book I had published, he wrapped it in brown paper so that nobody would be tempted to read it and be defiled, especially a woman, he said. But he was certain, as if I had told him, that that self-constructed person he had disliked had been torn down and his daughter, like Jairus's, raised up in one night.

That Puritan man knew, although I'm sure he would have denied it to himself and certainly to me, that I had committed a sin of which he entirely approved and would have said, but he had no words for it, or admissions of such a thing, "Don't look at it that way."

Had it not been for the approval of both our fathers, which we had sought so long, like lost twins, it might have remained a summer game.

The Bland House

There are always two stories, or maybe three, when you love, one private, one public, and a fairy story from the depths of childhood.

I know now that what I was entering was all three of these. There was not a nostalgia for the past alone, but a nostalgia for a present I would have lived had I not rejected that softer, more brutal place at eighteen. Maybe that is what romantic love is, a return to rejected possibilities, the illusion of a second chance, rooms turned gold, clothes turned silk and shimmering, people both larger and smaller, as in fairy tales, and the world benign. There are monsters in fairy tales, too, and children expect them, being more truthful, but not at the beginning of the story. That would be breaking the rules.

I used to look up from the tiny meadow outside the old barn, where at the crests of the two hills that formed barricades above it both our parents' houses stood. I did not know or care when I was fourteen, fifteen, sixteen, straining at the leash of my age and of the place, that they stood not only on their matching hilltops but were monuments to the same ambitions.

The Bland house was up beyond where the meadow turned to hillside. Mrs. Bland and her sister, who had been called Dearie ever since I could remember, and who came back to their garden from mysterious places from year to year, had had the hill terraced formally to tame it, all the way down to the edge of the meadow. I could see roses way in the distance, and thrust above them against the crest of the hill the long, stone balustrade of their terrace, like one of those hunting traps the mound builders made three thousand years ago above the valley.

The house had been built in 1916, when the coal business was booming in the First World War. Its mansard roof, its mullioned windows, its fieldstone walls made it look as if it glowered down on me.

My parents' house stood on the opposite hill, across the hollow, with its dirt road and its creek that ran only in spring. It, too, seemed like a fortress so far above me. Its garden, wilder and more lush, grew down their hill like wild woods toward a pool where my mother caught the creek water in spring and raised water lilies.

Its huge chimney, its red brick brushed with white, its dormer windows, and its terrace, gentler than the other, and opened to a border of evergreens that my father had brought down from the mountains, were all placed there in 1936. It had been the first Queen Anne house on the hill. My parents had gone, over and over, to the new reconstruction at Williamsburg, to make their own new past, measuring the woodwork, the dentils, the lintels of the doors, the size of the windows. It had taken my father ten years, after his return from the disaster in Kentucky, to corner enough of the valley money to build his own monument.

My parents' house was a fulfilled dream of my mother's, and the Bland house, at least the front of it, was certainly Mrs. Bland's. It had been everything in the world that she wanted, she said, and she added, At least at that time. She said that when Mr. Bland brought her all the way from Virginia—making it sound as if he had transported her across a winter sea, when she came from the first county in Virginia across the border, about three hours away—the only thing she insisted on was a house she could call her own, and not one other people had lived in, she was tired of that, family, don't you know, brought up in a house that had been there since 1876, but the foundations were much older. She wanted to start fresh, she said, and it had taken Mr. Bland ten years, too, to give her what she wanted.

So most of the house was a 1916 dream, the stone, the mansard roof, the mullioned windows. Dearie said, whenever it was talked about, and it was, often, that it looked like a seaside villa at Bournemouth, and Mrs. Bland always said, "What's wrong with that?"

Dearie would mutter, "If you don't know I can't tell you," and trudge out of the room.

Once there had been a wide encircling porch, which might have redeemed it, but Mrs. Bland had realized in 1936, looking across the hill at where Queen Anne was being resurrected on my parents' lot, that this was wrong, and had had it taken off and a small entryway with a Georgian door and lunette put in its place. She said she had restored the front, but not in front of Dearie.

But beyond the Georgian door, Mr. Partlow Bland, Charley's father, laid down the law. He stood five feet seven in his stocking feet. He had not gained a pound since he was a cadet at the Virginia Military Institute in 1900.

He was the only Gentile in Canona who had a subscription to *The New York Times*, and when I first went back, he welcomed me as if I were a messenger from some glamorous land he had left a long time ago or read about or paid to hear once a year at Carnegie Hall. That was in the first months, when the Bland family still thought I was "visiting." I was, to them, like Kierkegaard's wild goose, who stayed behind from the migration to help the tame geese learn to fly.

He liked to be entertained by whatever new blood Charley thought it wise to bring up from the town. When he heard the front door open, he would look up with the anticipation of a boy. Hope made his breath pause, until he saw who it was and, too often, it would deflate again. He was eighty years old.

So what I thought was that delicate time when a boy brings a girl home for approval was, like so much else, a form of family amusement. Charley brought me as a gift for his parents' evenings.

Mr. Bland was delighted. He showed it. He said, "My God, I can't believe you're the same little young'un used to hide in my barn." When he saw my surprise, he laughed. "Of course I knew. Used to change the hay for you. Wouldn't have let you know any more than a wild animal. Afraid of scaring you off." Then, dismissing the others, "*They* never knew."

He would look over my head at Charley and say, "Son, how in the hell did you do it?" It was one of the jokes between them, with its edge and then its depth of past criticism, that Charley had learned long since to live with. Sometimes I was caught in the cross fire. "He told me," Charley said, laughing with him, "that it was time I took a wife."

Mr. Bland broke in, a comedy act. "He said, Papa, whose wife do you have in mind?" They told this several times, laughing about it together, finding the story irresistible when I was sitting there waiting for Charley to speak for me. I did not realize then that the joke was descended from George Moore through Mark Twain to them.

Charley told me once that he had never pleased his father before that he could remember, and then he said, "Not at home, anyway. Sometimes when we were hunting together." Hunting was Charley's other word for life.

But even that was being invaded by Sadie, who was learning to shoot, as she did everything else, she said, "almost professionally." It made me think of mercenaries and hit men. She was going to a teacher in Aiken, South Carolina, twice a year for a two-week course in shooting skeet and tame birds. She made Cuddy go, too, although Charley said he was gun-shy.

To devil her, behind my back, but making sure that I would overhear him, Mr. Bland called me her sister-in-law. He called it that, deviling. He said he did it to get her goat. It was his favorite game in that evening time of quietness if not peace when, in summer, they sat on the terrace behind the house and had drinks from a silver tray, every evening the same—bourbon, water, ice, and peanuts. Mr. Bland said sane people had habits. It wasn't that you had habits, but what kind. The kinds of habits they had from five-thirty in the evening until they trudged off to bed were dictated by him, and for years they had not changed.

Dearie came down from the shrine of her room, smelling of gin. She hated bourbon and said so every evening, but nobody listened anymore, so she had long since fallen into saying little else. She tried once to use me to talk to as the others did, but when she found out I hadn't been anywhere, as she said, but Europe, she gave up.

For the rest of her time, she gardened and held long conversations with her own dog, a fourteen-year-old cocker spaniel that Mr. Bland couldn't stand the sight of. Sometimes I would see her, her wide behind upended among the lilies, or sitting way out over the hill in the afternoon, the dog asleep at her feet, as if she were an uninvited child. She and my mother were fond of each other. My mother said they spoke the same language. It consisted of talk about native shrubs and almost all of the weaknesses of mankind.

Mr. Bland insisted that the dogs be let out of the kennel where Mrs. Bland had exiled them all day. I think that he had a secret wish that they would eat Dearie's cocker spaniel, but he had trained them far too well for that. They lay on the stone floor at his feet. They watched him for approval, like the rest of the family did, except for Mrs. Bland, who, as she said, went her own merry way. He controlled the dogs with a click of his fingers, a wave of his hand, quietly, the way Bobby Low had done.

He taught me to do that, too, when I was given Jubal, a beautiful, tractable English setter whose spirit had been broken by a bad trainer.

He told me to bring Jubal so he could see how he was going, and when Jubal, at a finger click and a motion, lay down at my feet, he pointed this out to Sadie, who looked at me with a pure emotion—hate. Her retriever, Mosby, was one of those dogs that nobody could have trained, but Mr. Bland didn't excuse her for that. He just said she didn't know dogs, which, to someone else, would be like saying they didn't know their Bible.

Once in a while, Mosby would get out of his kennel and come galumping up the hill, stomping on the lilies and the frail columbine, all joy, knocking things over, until Cuddy caught him and took him home. He reminded me of Thurber's bear, who could take it or leave it alone. The other dogs didn't move.

That was in the summer. The Bland family stood for what I had learned to distrust as the most subtle kind of cruelty in the world, delicate genteel Gentile cruelty. I remembered being accused once by a friend of being born with a silver knife in my hand. "You don't even honor the people you destroy by hating them," he said, the you generic, "you just prune them like unwanted branches."

Yet, because I was in love, I accepted this and, after so many years of perception beyond it, retreated and took part in it. I say "in love" because profane love is a place, an Eden, a prison. Within it, people glow, colors are bright, you believe everything you have always wanted to believe. It is a place of trust, of guilelessness and deep iridescent illusion. I think the snake that seduced Eve was not temptation but guile, for it was the one quality that could destroy her.

I had been invited back at last. I was invited because they, in the guise of Charley, were bored, and I stayed because it was the happiest summer I had been offered since I was six years old.

For a little while we grew within the acceptance of his

father. Our father who art on the terrace making room for us at last in a house on a hill with a threadbare Oriental carpet and a flinging of dogs that I wouldn't be taken away from, not this time. Mr. Bland, in spite of the others, held a promise of that in his whole compact body and soul.

If the front of the house belonged to Mrs. Bland, the back belonged to Mr. Bland. He had insisted on what he called a parapet, and he would stand behind it like a general, he pronounced it jann-e-ral, and survey the river and the city as if he were going to attack. He called it a coign of vantage. The stone parapet reminded him of VMI, where he had gone as a state cadet because his family had no money after the war.

When he said "the war," he meant the Civil War, even though he had served as a colonel in the First World War; gone, as Mrs. Bland said, still disapproving, leaving her with two children to rear, when he was far too old. He had been in the Argonne Forest. He never said France. It was always the Argonne Forest.

From the parapet he looked down over the garden that fell away in a series of delicate beds and delicate colors like steep giant steps, where the women had tamed the hillside, as if Mrs. Bland wanted to remind him that no matter how tall he stood over the valley, commanding the city in the distance, she stood there between him and the river, and always would, no matter what he said.

Sometimes, before the others came out, we had a chance to stand there together. Down beyond the side garden, we could see the roof of Sadie and Cuddy's house, which had been my barn, and see the cars pass on the new road. Then Mr. Bland talked in a way I never heard him when anyone else was there. He told the truth as if it hardly mattered, and he told it to me because I had traveled, he said, and would understand. Only he called it "getting out." He made it sound like I had been sprung from a jail made of the surrounding mountains.

It was the only time he ever spoke with any kind of rawness. When he spoke, it wasn't to me, but in front of me, fragmented words that sprang out of his thought and then, usually before he even finished the sentence, retreated back into his silence again. Otherwise he protected himself with all the evasiveness of courtesy and wit, an old-fashioned country wit he used to rule them all, if only for the little while from five o'clock until bedtime.

We stood together, always in the same place, in the evening before the others gathered for "before-dinner drinks." They were careful not to say cocktails. Charley called it teatime to escape using the forbidden word. It was one of the unwritten rules of polite language they had picked up from somewhere.

Mr. Bland called it city language. "Hell's fire, the way they all talk," he said, nodding at the empty living room as if it were soon to be filled with people he didn't know very well. "Guests instead of company. Lunch and dinner instead of dinner and supper. City tacky. Sadie tells people we are related to the best families in Virginia, poor little ignorant thing. I told her we were kin to some white folks in Spotsylvania County, and distant at that. Related! Who ever heard tell.

"The commandant at VMI when I was there told us, 'Boys, I'm here to teach you engineerin' and command, but I don't want any boy leaving here talkin' better than his ma and pa. I don't know. Gentlemen then . . .'" and he stared at the river as if the gentlemen were spirits floating away in the prevailing wind that was pockmarking the bricks with chemical fumes from upriver.

"Her pa drank over the kitchen sink and mine locked himself in the upstairs front bedroom while Ma prayed and wept and wept and prayed in the parlor." Then he laughed as if he had defeated all of that a long time ago.

He would read the city below him from the river to the opposite mountain, where we could see the rows of tiny white dots that were tombstones in the cemetery. He called it a mean, malicious little town, and he would add sometimes, out of the blue, as he called it, "I got something on every damned one of them."

I could almost see his silence then as a place he went to and came back from. He had missed nothing in the years since he had come over the mountains from eastern Virginia to seek his fortune. He had become Canona's richest mine owner, had kept, as he said, his skirts clean of politics and most of the secrets he knew to himself.

He told me once, watching over the valley, his little claw hands with their perfect manicured nails—it was a vanity of his—resting on the parapet, "I swore to God I was going to come out here and make a place they couldn't get me out of." Who *they* was, he didn't say.

Once or twice, when he came back out of a long silence, he was in his childhood. "My uncle was already out here in the coal business. He had three daughters. They didn't give me the time of day." I knew the Bland girls, all long dead, from my own father's dreams of the girls in their white dresses that had formed his plan for my life.

"The worst thing that can happen to you in this vale of tears," Mr. Bland said to the trees, letting me hear, "is to be distant kin. I can buy and sell them now, and I'm still distant kin. Here"—he touched his neat lapel—"in myself. I swear to God to this very day, when I go back to Spotsylvania County I can feel myself begin to shrink at the border, and there ain't all that much of me in the first place." And when, after a while, he came back from thinking about Spotsylvania County, he said, "Sometimes I think it's the only real place I've ever known . . ."

"My pa lasted twenty years after the war, sitting on the porch in a rocking chair and mourning what he called the death of the South. Ma said he was a hero, but my grandam said he fit on both sides. That's the way she said it, with one of those eloquent Southrun lady snorts: 'He fit on both sides.' We had it as a joke, but not in front of Ma. She said she worshipped the ground he walked on. I had a picture. Handsome fellow. I don't remember him that way, though, like the picture. I just remember him sitting and rocking on the porch and reading the newspaper, and Ma saying, Don't bother your pa. He don't feel good. But in the picture he was a tall, fine-looking fellow. I just prayed to the Lord I would be tall and handsome like he was in that picture, but that was one of the many prayers the Good Lord didn't see fit to answer." Then he said, "Charley looks like that picture," and fell into his silence again.

"I found out later my grandam was right. He did fight on both sides. A lot of them did. They did it to get out of jail when the Yankees captured them. Then so many of them just came on home and retreated into a dream and the women had to do every damn thing. Grandam said she was glad he died, even if she did have to listen to my fool ma carry on. If there was one thing she couldn't stand it was a lazy man. She used to root me out from wherever I had hidden to get a little peace and quiet, and she'd switch my

legs with a willow and say, A great big boy like you settin'
down. I was about five years old then. She and Ma fought
like cats and dogs when they weren't having company. But
when I bragged, it was Ma's husband I bragged about, I
needed that, some good old brag. When there's not any
money you got to have some brag." Then, giving me useful
information, he said, "Willow switches are the best. Got
some play in them, *swish*.

"I was the man of the house when I was five years old.
They piled a heap of hopes on me, one little old shavetail.
We didn't have a red cent, but then, neither did anybody
else. We made out like it didn't make any difference, nice
people didn't have money, only people who would do anything to get it. It's a bad thing to want money with half
your soul and shame yourself with the other half for wanting it," he said once to the tops of the trees. "That's why I
swore . . ." and as usual, he left me to fill in the rest.

He turned what he had heard and remembered into
things that had happened to him, but they were not lies.
They were the Southerner's way of telling stories. It just all
sounded better to them when it had been commandeered,
transmuted, and made personal. They were, by their Southern nature, a *manqué* of novelists.

"When I was a little boy," he said, "I was walking along
a street in Lexington and I saw Marse Robert ride by on his
other horse, the one that is in the third basement down at
VMI. A lady was walking on the sidewalk across the street.
She was carrying a blue parasol. He stopped to tip his hat
to her. I can still see him, that handsome old man, maniacing
his horse with the foot she couldn't see so he would cut a
dash." He smiled at the memory and the river. But he had
been in Spotsylvania County when he was growing up, and

he had not been born until 1880 and "Marse Robert" was dead then and it had been another little boy.

Mr. Bland provided the habit of family cruelty that passed as wit and that they all copied, Charley with the natural style he had in everything he did, and Cuddy awkwardly; he never quite chose the right social wound to pour the salt into, although he tried. At the same time, within the confines of a set of concrete manners, Mr. Bland was belligerently without prejudice, as conservative men of his generation were. He told me once about meeting Booker T. Washington on the train from Canona to Palmyra. He was always specific about details in his stories, whether they were true or not. "I shook his hand because I admired him, but I didn't take my hat off," he explained.

His best friend in the world—he always spoke of him that way, "my best friend in the world, Harry Goldstein"— was his lawyer. When he tried to get Harry into the Canona Country Club, which he and Mrs. Bland had helped start, so he and Harry could play golf together, Harry was voted down by three members of the board. He didn't even bother to name them. "New money" was all he said. It had happened thirty years before, but the phrase still sounded like the wrath of God.

He had two places he went to every year alone—or he said it was alone, meaning that it wasn't with Mrs. Bland. He went to the Seniors Tournament at Egeria Springs. He and Harry went to New York every winter and stayed from the time the FFV got to Pennsylvania Station on Friday morning until the *George Washington* left on Sunday evening. They stayed at the Biltmore—he said that that was where Southerners always stayed—and went to four concerts. They went to a concert on Friday night, a Saturday matinee, one Saturday night, and one on Sunday afternoon.

They went, as they always had, to Carnegie Hall. They wrote ahead for the same seats, since over the years they had found out where the acoustics were best. Once in 1938, he said, they had heard Toscanini conduct Beethoven, but I didn't know if that was one of his stories or not.

Mrs. Bland said, "I'm glad he's got someone to go with." She told me he insisted on Harry Goldstein and his fat wife being asked to dinner once a year, and said they always came, with a little complicit smile.

"I let it go on," Mr. Bland said once, just at twilight. "I was too damn busy to stop it, and by the time I noticed, it was too late." Whether it was the treatment of Harry Goldstein and his fat wife, or the general state of affairs, I never knew.

His voice stopped without finishing, as it usually did. Then he said, "They're my own damned fault. Put them out here on the edge of money . . ." Who *them* was he didn't need by then to say at all.

"The Bible admonishes us to love one another, but it don't say a damned thing about *like*," he said once, glaring at the still empty living room.

From time to time he tried to warn me, not looking at me but reading the future in the treetops he stared at while I watched his hands on the stone, and the warnings, too, I had to piece together and remember when he was no longer there.

"Ever since that boy was born she's been treating him like the prodigal son. Forgives him every Saturday night. Hell, to be a prodigal son you got to *go someplace*. Charley just goes downtown. Who ever heard of a prodigal who never left home? Let me tell you something. She likes him the way he is. Gives her something to think about all the time. Gives her power, too. Rather have him home drunk than someplace else sober." He patted my hand, which I had left on the parapet beside his, and said, "Damn. You're the prodigal, honey, you had some get-up-and-get, and they'll never forgive you for it."

Whatever else he was going to say that time, and for once he hadn't stopped in mid-sentence or mid-thought, was stopped by Sadie, who strode onto the terrace looking tall and still telling Cuddy over her shoulder something she wanted him to do. She didn't bother to speak to me, and Mr. Bland grinned like an imp.

Later, Mr. Bland forgot all that and told me that Charley had been picked as the family bachelor. "I swear I think she did it before he was born," he said. "Had him as the second son, gave me Cuddy. I don't even like Cuddy. He copies everything I do. I can't blow my nose in front of Cuddy. She raised Charley to look after her in her old age, she said so, like an insurance policy, and she's never seen a damn thing wrong with doing that to somebody. Bred him for it. I don't know what the hell she thought I was doing."

He said Southern families did that, forgetting that he had been a friend of my own uncle, who had suffered the same fate, even to being cast as a devil with the ladies, until he shot himself in his secretary's bedroom, which was part of the expected role.

But he hadn't forgotten him. "Mighty high rate of suicide with those men, honey, mighty high. I never have been able to figure out why. Don't ever take a damn bit of responsibility."

He said people were wrong to think Southern bache-
lors were fairies; it wasn't that. Most of them weren't worth
a hill of beans, but they were lovable, which was part of the
role, and they were damned convenient, usually good with
dogs. He said that Charley had all the makings.

Then he was quiet for a while and I thought he wasn't
going to say any more, but he was. He was thinking of his
own uncle, he said, who had given them the living-room
carpet that he made Mrs. Bland keep. He had brought it
back from someplace in the East. "He was out there for a
long time," he told me. "He fought for the Khedive of Egypt,
like a lot of Confederates did who didn't want to swear the
loyalty oath after the war. My grandam always said that after
the amnesty he brought home as loot everything that wasn't
nailed down." He said that Dearie had been cast as the
maiden aunt—miscast," he added, laughing. There was always one of those, too, in Southern families.

"Don't forget, not a day has passed when Charley
couldn't have stood up and walked out that door. That was
another thing I prayed for. Don't let that momma-clinging
fool you. Men like that have lazy souls. Momma is an excuse.
Oh, I don't know, maybe that's too hard on Charley. Habit
forges mighty strong chains. But I swear to God, I've seen
her take him coffee and the paper morning after morning
when he was too damned lazy to get up. It was like something you find in the funny papers. I used to walk down to
my office sick at my stomach. But who is going to walk away
from never having to pay the electric bill?" He grinned.
"You're like all the rest. You'll listen, but you won't hear.
Why don't you find a man who's worth the trouble?"

I thought, He is talking about his own son and he hates
him too much, and I wanted to tell him that Charley was

waiting for a sign from him more than from her, and I denied what he said, but later his voice stayed to sustain me, a rock-hard saving grace. The evenings at the parapet became, for me, as timeless as they are today.

While I still rejected what he was saying as much as I could, he had made me see them all from another angle, as if a camera had been turned on them from the backside of their lives. "She's a hard woman," he said about Mrs. Bland. He smiled to soften what he was telling me, even as he said it. "I had me an old dog, I loved that old bitch— the dog, I mean—no more hunt in her; she had long since earned her place on the living-room carpet. I went to New York one weekend with my best friend, Harry Goldstein, and she had my dog put down. Said the smell was 'unpleasant.' Unpleasant! You don't even use that word around a dog. Just killed my dog because it was old and smelly and in the way."

We stood there in those few calm minutes all the summer, looking across Mrs. Bland's barrier of tulips, and then of roses, and then of lilies, until there was, as my father always said, a smell of fall in the air. The chrysanthemums had begun to bloom, and things to change.

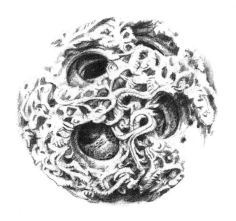

The Small Corner

The evening belonged to Mr. Bland, but the afternoon was Charley's mother's. She, too, wanted to be amused, but in her own way, at her own time, and I, because Charley knew better than I that she had to be placated, turned up, as she wanted me to that summer, almost every afternoon. She would wait and watch for me in the same chair where I still see her after nearly thirty years, waiting for Charley in the night.

When I went in, she would be playing solitaire because she had finished *The New York Times* long since. She read it at the same time every day, to keep up with the world. She had folded it carefully and put it beside her magazines, where Mr. Bland need only reach a hand up from the chair that became his in the evening. Imogene, their maid, told me once that she had asked for it to be pressed, and Imogene told her she wasn't going to do anything of the kind.

Mrs. Bland talked about "the servants" as if there were a whole household, but there was only Imogene, who had been there since she was sixteen and was now fifty-three, and whose given name was Evelyn, but Mrs. Bland said she called her Imogene because all her maids had been called that ever since the first one who really was, Imogene, don't you know, back in Virginia. It was easier than having to change. She said Imogene said, "My goddamn name is Evelyn."

She went to the Institute three nights a week after she cleaned up their dinner. They ate early because they understood, but Mrs. Bland said she ought to learn something practical, not waste her time and theirs with all those English courses. Imogene was a vociferous reader, she said, as if she were a child prodigy.

Then there was Randolph, who worked in the yard, but who was commandeered from time to time to put on a white coat and stumble around. He liked to stop me whenever he saw me and tell me, he said, what was going on. He said he thought I ought to know.

Mrs. Bland, too, was lightly in love for the present with the middle-aged girl who was myself, but she did not know this, or care. She only knew that she waited for me to come, almost every day at the same time, to lift the boredom, which she thought of as tranquillity, to bring her a glimpse of those places and those things she longed to go back to sometime— the books, the European cities.

The rug where her feet rested had been brought back from Kerman in Iran, when it was Persia, years before by Dearie, in the days when she was, as she called herself, a virgin traveler. She said a *hadj* had knelt on it for prayers, and this comforted Mrs. Bland. She explained the pointed arch of its design to me and said it ought to face east, toward Mecca.

Beside her, on the wide windowsill, she kept her special magazines, her *Connoisseur*, her *Antiques*. She asked these of Charley every Christmas and she said he never failed her, never forgot to send in the thing you send in. It was a habit she took pride in, as in most of her habits, a part of her, sometimes she told me, making fun of herself; she thought her habits were all that was left of her, like a corn husk without the ear of corn. She took pride, too, in thinking like that, in admitting that she was a country girl.

But more than all the rest on the windowsill, the magazines, the folded paper, the perpetually unfinished needlepoint, the cards, the mah-jongg set, all the things you have in living rooms, she took pride in her "pearl of great price," her devil's work ball.

It sat on a black carved Chinese plinth, the carved ivory puzzle ball Dearie had brought so long ago from China. "Well, actually," Mrs. Bland told me, "she bought it in Hong Kong, but she says it came, the man swore this, from the Imperial Court of the last Empress, and it is made from the most valuable part of the tusk, called Great Ivory, of the wild African elephant, not those tame ones you see in India. Sometimes, don't you laugh, I can hold it in my hand and stare at it until I see the great elephant from Africa looming there against the sky above the terrace, and then to come to this, well, so are the mighty fallen."

She told me that when she saw the actual African elephants from the balcony of the lodge in Kenya, the one the Queen went to, don't you know, she was disappointed. They were smaller than the great bull of her visions, but then they were quite far away, almost toys.

Charley Bland

Dearie told her that in the Imperial Court the carver worked on it until he went blind. "I can see and feel the connection, don't you know?"—her favorite phrase she had picked up someplace that was not where they were brought up. "I mean with the real Imperial Court. Did you know that the Dowager Empress took a different young lover every single night and then had them killed in the morning? Good grief, and here it all is, right in my hand. Think of that," she said, and paused for a catch of silence, thinking of it, "a man who would give his eyesight for art, and a beautiful young soldier, at least I see him as a soldier." Artist and lover have touched it, as she has touched it, sensing them both, the old blind carver and the handsome young soldier who will die.

Sometimes, almost as a duty, she would hold the devil's work ball in her hands, stroking the lace-like ivory carvings of its insane dragons, and show me, one ball within another, more insane dragons turning inward, spheres within spheres within spheres.

"Life," she told me, "can be like that, all the complications turning inward on themselves; well, at least there is safety in it, and that is important, after all." She said she had been every place you could name, but for years, she had sat in the corner of her living room in the afternoon and would be there, she was certain, until she died. "No matter what plans we make," she told me, "I won't get any farther than New York."

What was between us in this little arena of faded chintz, a window, a prayer rug, a worn carpet which she said she hated, the Victorian chair which had been designed for crinolines to fall over its sides but had long since turned into the chair I sat in to be questioned, either by her or by Mr.

Bland? Often there was nothing to say, and I could hear a breeze lift the corner of *The New York Times*.

We sat in the small corner of a room, but in worlds apart. The love we shared, or had in common, was for Charley Bland, but the power, the concentration, the energy was among the women—Mrs. Bland, Dearie, Sadie, and myself; they on one side, I on the other of some silk rope in a tug of war, and he was made into the object, the prize.

What did I ask of her, this woman who looked into *The New York Times* in order, she said, to talk to Mr. Bland, but they never did, not anymore?

She read mild, well-written domestic books, what I called, to myself but not to her, the chinaberry school of Southern writing. Perceptive little gems about families were what she liked best, but she saw no excuse for being explicit about sex. She had read them all, and she sought, she said, wit, and wanted books with plots about people with enough money so she didn't have to think about it, but witty, well written, don't you know. She liked to talk about literature, but not at dinner, where she said that what moved her was not understood.

She wanted to be friends, casually, in the afternoon, and after that time of the day she wanted me to go—out of her mind, out of her room, out of her son's life, too, when they tired of me as they had the others who had gone before me. She told me this, with that awful honesty that showed she didn't care what I knew. It was all the same to her. "It will be, for us, and in time for him, as simple as the closing of a door. It always is."

She was able from long experience to judge the tensile weakness that she could recognize. She tried to explain it to me, as coolly as if I were a bystander, gossiping, abstractly, speaking of her son, who had no name when she mentioned these things. "My son," she said, as if I didn't know who he was, "is far too attractive to marry anybody." She used the word "my" as she did when she talked about her devil's work ball.

"Sex," she said, speaking of women's things but not before the men, not ever, "doesn't really last long, and when that is over, what do you have?" The word "marriage" hung between us and she brushed it aside like a cobweb. She knew, and said—she prided herself on not being afraid to say what she thought and believed—another favorite word, that she gave her son everything he needed except that one thing, making a category of our love, like the time of day, the Lapsang-souchong tea, our secret lives, which were no secret but a convenience for the time being, but which she did not take too seriously.

She had always succeeded in having what she wanted, and it made her more dangerous than anyone I have ever known. She used charm like a blunt instrument.

My own mother scorned the warmth I had sought, it seems, forever, leaving me vulnerable to charm. She was colder, less politely brutal, more honest, and less strong in these ways of convenience because she had always been too proud to use seduction as a weapon. She had succeeded in her intention to make me come back to the valley, which she intended when she planned all this so quickly, seizing her chance in the parking lot, using Charley to call me home as if I were a dog whistled back.

My mother and Mrs. Bland, although they didn't like each other very much, had lived for years as mirror images across the narrow defile of the hills, each in her separate stronghold, with the gardens they showed during Garden Week, laughing about the people who paid to come.

I wanted this cold, seductive woman in the corner of a suburban room to love me in a way she didn't know or, if she did, would not have done. I set out, day after day, on the road of brass that I took to go there, to see that frail old girl, ponderous and powerful, and dared not tell the truth to her. I was afraid. I had been trained to be afraid. My fault was fear, my sacrifice to her was Charley, who feared her more than I did, and begged me to wait on her, as on an early summer day that I remember, when the roses were blooming outside the French doors to the terrace.

I had brought all my longings and my study in other places as a sacrifice to this small time of fear in the afternoon, this frail-bodied woman with scratches down her freckled arms.

She said, "I was attacked by a rose. I think it heard me."

I have made a monster of her because I could not bear her indifference. She did not care. She simply did not care. She knew the time would pass and I would go, and there would be, with her, a decent glow of satisfaction that nothing had changed, sameness had been shored up for another day, and she would put Campho-Phenique on her arm and say it was nothing, meaning it.

"I was walking by the rose, and I said to my sister, 'It has to go. It takes up too much room, and I don't care if it is called Queen Elizabeth, it looks like Jean Harlow to me,' and it reached out and scratched me. Dearie says they can hear and feel, roses. They are supposed to be sacred to the Virgin Mary," she said, "but I don't think so."

She rubbed her clawed arm and suggested that we have

tea. It was my cue to make it, each day the same. Because I had lived so long in England, she said, I made it well, and she decided that I missed what she called the ceremony, and told me again about going to Trumper's, where her hostess was distantly related to an earl, a belted earl, she said with the same smile every time she told me.

The Attic

For three weekends every year at the same time Mrs. Bland went away. There was the weekend when the ladies who were restoring the house met on the farm where Lee's horse, Traveller, had been foaled. Mrs. Bland said she wasn't fooled for one minute about the importance of that, but it was the only historic house they could find that hadn't already been restored to its rafters, to a way it had never been in the first place, and then added, with a grin, "like all of us jumped-up farm girls puttin' on." It was the grin and the recognition that she knew, and had always known, what she was doing, that gave her her strength, and her wit, made her step down to being likable, easygoing, younger, as if for a little while she had unfrozen a secret part of herself and was sharing it with me.

The moment passed, a glimpse, that was all, of the girl amused at the woman she had become, and she added that some of her friends from Virginia went to what they had named Traveller's Rest, and it was free and the food was wonderful and they always had the meeting when the gardens were at their best. She could bring back ideas, she said, for Dearie to plant—historic ones.

At the same time, Dearie, who had picked up the nickname from an English friend who had visited and had been the only English person not to be invited back, went to stay with a friend who lived in Connecticut, unless one of Mr. Bland's two dogs was sick and then Mrs. Bland said it needed Dearie. Otherwise she told Dearie she needed to get away.

Dearie's friend raised prize dahlias that Mrs. Bland wouldn't allow her to bring back to plant in the garden, even though she did most of the work, her wide behind as familiar on the giant steps as the frailer, more genteel flowers that would, according to one of the perpetual family truisms they all seemed to live by, grow for Dearie and for nobody else. Mrs. Bland said the dahlias were too bright, too big, too, oh, troubling, fighting for the word and finding it as if she hadn't said it before, according to Dearie, every time Dearie went to Connecticut.

What she really meant, as Dearie told me once, peeking out like a little girl from behind her haven of gin to see how I would take it, was that she couldn't stand Dearie's friend, who was, she said confidentially, knowing, she put it that way, that I would understand, a dyke that weighed 250 pounds and was too bright, too big, far too colorful. She was rich and tended to take Dearie to places like the Yucatán and Machu Picchu, and had once taken her around the world. Dearie said most of those places were shit, her shit to be exact. She'd had Montezuma's and Atatürk's and Lao-tzu's and Brahma's revenge more times than she could say and hadn't lost a pound; she wished to hell she'd take her to Paris, which she hadn't seen since '29, but then beggars couldn't be choosers.

Then there was the weekend that Mr. Bland and Mrs. Bland went together on the show plane to New York. Then, she said, it was her turn to choose what they saw, but they did go to the opera, not just to musicals and commercial plays. She said she was starved for that kind of thing. Mr. Bland insisted on going once to the ballet. He said he liked to see those damn girls toe-dance.

The spiritual weekend happened in early June. Mrs. Bland said that the wild azaleas in the mountains were at their height and absolutely lovely. She went for that weekend to a conference at the Episcopal Center in the North Carolina mountains (so she would see them). She drove herself so she could stop whenever she wanted to; she said it made her feel free. Charley always offered to drive her, but she said, "Don't be silly, you'd be bored to death." She went every year, she said, and smiled, a little embarrassed to be talking about such things in such a way, to cleanse her soul.

It happened, and maybe it was coincidental, at the same time that one of the seniors' tournaments was held at Egeria Springs, so it was convenient for Mrs. Bland to pray for spiritual guidance and discuss what the Scriptures really meant, while Mr. Bland played golf.

Each time Mrs. Bland went away, the silver was put under the sofa and the guest-room bed. Her treasures went to their bedroom floor under the tester bed she'd ordered from Williamsburg. They had been put in a velvet-lined box she said belonged to her grandmother in Virginia and had been buried when the Yankees came. Dearie said it was nothing of the kind, she bought it in a rummage sale in 1936, she remembered the day even, and Mrs. Bland said, "Dearie, don't say things like that. People will believe you."

Into the box went the Chinese devil's work ball that Dearie had brought her from Hong Kong, the copies of *Antiques* and *Connoisseur*, the alabaster bud vases, the bits and pieces of jewelry she thought would not be what she called *apra poh* for a spiritual weekend. She put in the brass candlesticks from the living-room mantel, which she had been calling a chimneypiece ever since she had read Nancy Mitford, so that nobody in West Virginia knew what she was talking about. She added, always at the last minute, holding it in her hand to decide, the little picture of her mother in the silver sweetheart frame, a very pretty woman under a puffed mound of hair. "She," her aged daughter said, her voice lowered properly, "was a Dunne." All of the necessary wedding and family photographs went into the velvet-lined box, too, imitation Bachrach in their imitation-Tiffany frames.

She had stood gazing at the living-room carpet while the men from the cleaners rolled it up for its yearly cleaning and moth treatment and said once again that she didn't like it, but Mr. Bland said it was fine, it was what he was used to. Besides, he thought new carpets were tacky, like you'd just made your money in the coal business.

Aristocracy in the valley had to do with when you made your money or, according to Mr. Bland, how long ago you had lost it. He said this once to Sadie, who had taken to making sniping attacks about when my family came back to the valley. "Her grandfather was driving a four-in-hand when yours were eating white beans," he told her, reveling in the fact that I was there to hear him.

I would not really have noticed most of the family treasures that Mrs. Bland hid with such care—they were conventional, and in every house of people like her—except for their seasonal absences, which made the house look somehow smaller, less personal, as if it had been deserted by its own legends.

It reminded me of playing with my cousin when we were children, in a long-deserted hospital on my uncle's property at Corona Mine. We climbed in a broken window and skidded along the corridors of dust, our voices hollow in the empty spaces. We found forgotten cups and saucers and trays and bedpans, and pretended to nurse patients in the rooms where the sun was fading in the broken windows through dirty veils of air.

When my father heard this he said, so I would stand up straight, "Your Aunt Mary, who you were named after, died on the second floor in the end room on the river side. She was only nineteen years old, but she was too tall and ruined her posture by slumping, and she destroyed her lungs and caught galloping consumption."

What he did not say or know was that her brothers, including himself, had killed her with ridicule. They told her she would never get a husband, not with that height, not with those feet. My mother said she would have been a beautiful woman, but not in 1912. I used to pretend to nurse her. There she lay for me on the empty stained mattress on a rusted cot left there, her face turned to the wall in deepest grief, but she looked lovely dying, with her long auburn hair like mine.

When Mrs. Bland went away, the house she ruled was like the deserted hospital, faded and sun-dusted, as if a tap of energy had been turned off and it had been left to die.

Charley Bland

She said that she had put enough silver out so that Charley could have dinner there if he wanted to, and perhaps, she told me with one of her twinkles, have a guest. She had, without saying so, left me to look after Charley while she was gone, a son-sitter.

So on the spiritual weekend in June when Mrs. Bland drove to North Carolina and Mr. Bland drove to Egeria, Dearie flew off to Connecticut, complaining that it was the wrong time to leave the garden. The house was left to us to pretend in, as if we were children.

I got there first, in the late afternoon, when it was safe to bring in food for the weekend. I brought carefully chosen clothes, as if I had packed for a honeymoon. I thought of it that way, amused at myself, and then, in the middle of the packing, burst into tears, which came so easily then, as if I were not allowed to miss a hint, not a nuance, in order to pay my dues for the happiness I was snatching in fits and starts and bits and pieces.

I tried to ignore both the bare floor and the empty sideboard where the tea service usually stood. I cut fresh roses and set them there, and set the table in the dining room with my own candlesticks.

He came in as soon as he could from the other world in the city; I knew it was soon, because we usually met in that pause between the demands of work and the demands of home, where we had a home of our own for a little while among the men who lingered, as he had done for so many years, at the Elks or the Moose or the Wayfaring Stranger, to breathe a little before anybody said anything they didn't want to hear.

He was as aware as I was of the time and the place, as if it were new to him, not bare, not without treasures. He looked around the house he had been born in as if it were newly blessed. He wandered around among the flowers I had found. He went into the kitchen, where I had the dinner nearly ready and the wine cooling. He said, "I don't even want to drink this evening," as if he was surprised at himself and at me.

He held me for a long time and said he had been longing to come home all day, home, really home, he said. We stood in the middle of the bare floor, and he smelled of that mixture of good tobacco and clean linen that had meant safety for me ever since Bobby Low had held me close to him when I was five, safety of the senses, the most deceptive safety in the world. I heard his live heart beating.

We sat on the terrace in the evening light, and we drank a glass of wine, playing at living there, but not using those words. We made it real, stolen but real for a little while, and I thought, when he had gone to change a Chopin record I had brought and he had said he liked when we played it at my apartment, that the glimpses of new light in his face, and the new beauty when he turned toward the evening, made it worth the cost, a rescue of a man so deep within the man so well liked and so little known. I saw him in strata like the strata that show on a cut cliff, not separate personalities, but hidden layers of hurt and joy he was trusting me enough to allow to come out into the twilight.

Charley said that when he drove into the driveway and heard the music haunting the air, it was the happiest time we could have, when we could wake up together. He said he had longed for that. It was one of the formal moments in our time together that I had learned to expect and accept, like a milestone in our evening. He used the word "long," "longed," or "longing," instead of "love." "I've longed for you," he said, every time, as if I had come back from a place he couldn't go to.

They were a family of repeaters, as if their opinions were archival, formal phrases for formal situations that had to be said every time. It wasn't verbal laziness. It was a statement of existence; they were the people who said those things and it made them somehow more real (in the best sense—a family phrase) than other people, a part of a myth that they had to create as they went along in order not to fade into oblivion.

The music echoed differently through the empty spaces; it floated from the living room unmuted, when we sat for a long time over our dinner until the night came down, and the fireflies were outside the windows, and each of us waited for the other to say it was time for bed.

Finally I went into the kitchen to clean up. He said we ought to, in case. What it was in case of, we both knew, and had since we were children—in case we were caught. Neither North Carolina nor Egeria Springs was far enough away to put out the fear within. I could see the lights of my parents' house out of the kitchen window, and knew that they knew where I was and didn't care, so long as it kept me in the city and not, as my father said, wandering off half-cocked.

Late and half through the night when the moon rose and was high and was gone, he slept on in the bed he had always been in, where his body fell at last into its habits, but we had made love there, and he said it was the first time he could remember that he had been sober, completely sober. For us to touch each other, to fall close upon each other, was not lustful but an extension of the language of love by other means. It was a growing together into body bloom, into the yes we lived no other time, not in public, not in the fear that kept us apart.

I didn't know then that he used that fear as his protection against the bursts of life he could hardly bear, as if rehearsals for ecstasy were needed to bear the weight of it. Lovemaking had before, to him, been a technique, a game, a pleasure, and a hunt, but never this, he said. What this was he had no need to say. I think I lay there beside him, cool and weightless, most of the night; I can still, after so long, see the night outside the windows of his room, sense the relief I had then of being alone and safe with him and him asleep. The final act of trust is not lovemaking; lust can drive you there. It is to lay down your arms and sleep, unprotected. Sleep then is a brave act, lying awake floating in a joy you might lose is braver. I must have slept at last, because he woke me with orange juice in the morning. We both moved as softly as our own shadows, not out of fear anymore, but in peace.

Charley and I even pretended to take each other for granted, which we could seldom do. He went to play golf on Saturday as he always did. We had the luxury of not planning, of something happening as it did for married couples, just for one weekend.

I sat in the chair that Mrs. Bland was always in when I came to tea and Mr. Bland sat in to read the *Times*. I think I thought that if I did what they did, I could also think for a minute as they did and begin to understand.

I found out only one thing. The chair looked straight out the front door, so that no one could come near the house without being seen. What I had thought sometimes was Mrs. Bland's poetic trance when she stared into the distance was her watch on the driveway to see who was coming.

I was reading Martin Buber's *I and Thou*, one of those books that sad women keep by their bedside. It was during this time of love that I read them all, Jung, Buber, Kierkegaard, trying to find some words to tell me that what was happening to me had happened before and that there was a way out without the sin of leaving things unfinished.

What I read was, I see now, far too profound for the shallow waters I was wading in, self-hypnotized into believing that the family that held me was somehow deeper, refusing to admit that I had been caught in a banal trap. I sank into trying to understand why I was there at all, in a stretched, still Saturday afternoon in June, in a place where I had done nothing, and was allowed to do nothing, not plant a flower or choose a plate, a magazine, an ashtray.

Instead, for a little while, I had been chosen, treated like the flowers or the Chinese ball or the vases from other, more exotic places—an object to be enjoyed or thrown away when they were tired of it or made a part of the legend.

I remembered Jung's dream of the depth of his past in a cellar of his dream house. There was no cellar, or I would have explored it first when I was left alone there. The rock cliff was the base of the house, so that whatever secrets there were that might have helped me to understand had to be someplace else.

I sat there in the mild afternoon, afraid to move, or to find out anything, and yet drawn, not to the nonexistent basement, but to the attic. I had seen the pull-down ladder leading to a painted square in the upstairs hall ceiling, or to somewhere, or nowhere in one of those dreams where you start climbing and can't get off and you have to keep on climbing into dark space, the ladder rungs disappearing behind you.

Like Bluebeard's wife, and Pandora, and all the other women who sit and wait for the courage to do what they want to, I was thrust toward it by curiosity. I knew, as I knew I shouldn't pull the ladder down, that it was haunted.

I wanted to find secrets that would tell me where I was, relics of a time when there might have been events instead of habits, decision, daring, Confederate death, scandal, something they were either retreating from or longing for, something to break the total lack of tension, someone they didn't talk about who'd been brave or ecstatic or unhappy or disgraceful.

What I hoped for was the saving grace of anger or the tragedy that can't exist without recognition, or some silent terror that I could understand, not the dread suspicion that their lives were no deeper than a fashion and a daily round that Mrs. Bland would kill for. They had made a castle of acceptance, but by whom and of what? I had been brought up in a more arrogant atmosphere, so I was disarmed in the face of that shallow yearning. I longed to find a bitten bullet, the teeth marks still on it.

I leaned against the ladder to keep from falling, and thrust the wooden square upward. It groaned as if the whole house were hurt. Finally it clicked upright in the yawning space. My head was just above the floor level of the attic; it must have seemed disembodied, propped there on the floor, but there was no one to see it, and had not been for a long time.

The long, low room disappeared beyond the light into dark places where the roof met the bare floor. It was lined with trunks, some with faded labels on them, labels from cities and hotels in Europe and what they would have called "the East," meaning New England, not China or Japan, some with school names painted on them—the various prep schools that they had sent Charley to; VMI, where his brother had gone. The metal foot locker nearest me had Mr. Bland's name, rank, and serial number from the First World War painted on it, dim and hard to read under the dust.

They stretched in rank and file into the half dark, trunks no longer used, seatless chairs, a broken bridge lamp, an old Victrola, an outdated Kodak, polo sticks propped in a corner, a sidesaddle with a pummel, a gun rack with no guns in it, a cutout picture of King Edward VIII when he was Prince of Wales, headless frail skeletons of dress forms, forgotten games and jigsaw puzzles, and the dry smell of death.

Birds chortled under the roofbeams; a squirrel scuttled across the roof. I made myself climb up and stand where the ceiling rafters were just higher than my head, and I watched the dust dance in streaks of sun. A little afternoon breeze came through the window, which had been left open an inch or so for ventilation. There were rain streaks on the sill, and a dead bird, dried, lay on the floor below it, and beside the bird, the shed skin of a snake.

I could see over the lawns and hillsides of the dream houses all the way to the upriver bend, as if I were flying over the slates of the roofs, looking down on the tops of the dogwoods, the magnolias, the genteel shrubs, the pachysandra, the tea roses of June, not a blowsy althea or a riotous lilac in sight, and no American Beauties. I saw my mother, sitting as she so often sat, in one of the white wrought-iron chairs by the pool in her garden, staring into space, listening to something she couldn't tell about. She had been doing that since I was a small child, and I learned never to interrupt her, for she would look at me when I pulled her sleeve as if I were a stranger. I backed away from the window. Somehow, even at that distance, I was afraid she might look up and wonder who I was.

There was a terrible tidiness all around me. I knelt and creaked open the cedar chest by the window. I hoped there would be ball gowns and scandals, pre-Civil War dresses, 1912 hats, lace jabots, tiny kid gloves in tissue paper, scented letters, and old dolls, like in the trunk I had found in my grandmother's house that my aunt had long since thrown away in a fit of family hatred.

The dress that lay on the top, wrapped in tissue paper, was gray georgette with a white voile fichu embroidered with tiny pink roses, a true dress of the twenties, not the fringed frolics that are part of nostalgia. I had opened a haunted box, but it was my own whispers, not theirs, that I released. I heard the small children playing on Mrs. Grieves's porch, and the breeze that let the swings creak behind the green-and-white-striped awnings that made a deep shade on an afternoon before anyone had lost their money. There were the murmured voices of the grownups somewhere above me. I found myself hoping, as I had then, that nobody would move or change anything.

The trunk next to it was smaller, and when I opened it, it was so full that photographs fell out and slid across the floor like thrown cards; Bachrach backlit photographs of women and girls from the early thirties, when their hair was tightly waved, through the late thirties, when it climbed high on their foreheads and flowed down their backs, some enlarged snapshots, one dewy-eyed in front of a duck blind, several in riding clothes, in hunting clothes, in evening clothes, and one, stuck behind another in its tarnished silver frame and fallen out just enough for me to pull it free, stark naked and grinning. It was Kitty Puss Baseheart when she was what everybody called a fast young girl, pert and cute, her hands clasped behind her head, her lips bee-stung. I was ashamed of the intrusion and put it back behind the picture of a woman in a twin sweater set and pearls, smiling slightly, as people were told to do then they had their pictures taken. The photographs had in common the browning of age from sepia to dark spots like the spots on old hands. They were a WASP chronicle of a lost woman's world. They had youth and slim acceptable Protestant faces, a steady watchfulness at the camera or whoever was looking at the image, a reminder that they, relegated to a box in the attic, had existed, and had been in love with Charley Bland.

All of them were signed the same way, a caprice of his. He had asked me to do the same thing, and I had thought it was so private. I knew then that for his seductions he hadn't even changed his tunes, the evasive promises of the wild colonial boy that if you did make the bed and light the light, he just might stop by late at night, Blackbird, bye, bye . . . All signed . . . *I'll be home, love, all love, dearest love, I'll never forget, think of me*, all pleas, all hopes, and a series of fashions in names from the time girl children were named for flowers through the last-names-first phase to Lisa and Carol. A photograph of me with my setter dog, Jubal, sat on his dresser, signed the way he had asked for it.

I caught a glimpse of myself in thrall, in durance vile, like that lady who got pushed down the stairs in one of the Waverley Novels. I forget who she was. My mother had read it to me when I was too small to choose for myself. I saw myself caught there until I, too, was relegated to the attic among the photographs, because that was the rule of real, or was it true, love—that you see it through to the end or to the happy-ever-after he seemed to have promised them all. I hadn't known how deep his wound was, how unfinished the man. He wanted more than his famous seductions, he wanted love, and he had wanted it and received it from all of them and it had never been enough.

I told myself in the dusty attic what they all had said sometime or other—not me, though, not me, not this time; I am not like the others, that legion of clinging hopeful women—and told myself the answer to that in my grandmother's voice, "Don't be a bigger damned fool than you are already."

The telephone rang far away, a hollow ring in the empty house below, and rang and rang until it stopped and the silence closed in again. I think I turned and opened the trunk behind me, still kneeling, to get away for a minute from those playing cards of women on the floor.

It had belonged to Dearie before she was cast by the family as the sweet old-maid aunt who tended the roses and the dogs. Here was a place that Mrs. Bland's ominous definitions had not invaded.

Flung, not lain or wrapped, just abandoned on the top of a pile of clothes were two little foxes with their teeth sunk in each other's tail. I thrust my hands into the "fur piece" like the one my father had finally been able to afford to give my mother one Christmas during the Depression, and I saw a vision, a vision of Paris in the twenties, of elegant stern women sitting at sidewalk cafés, in costumes by Worth or Chanel, Parma violets pinned to their shoulders with diamond brooches, cloche hats that were as straight as kepis,

and furs like these thrown over their shoulders—fur pieces
to be copied later by the ladies of the American South.

Women, a world of women, solid women, Buddha
women, long-legged, Leonor Fini women in thigh boots, the
strung muscles of their calves straining against Italian
leather—that was the clutched vision of the fur in the hot
attic in the afternoon, as out of place in these residues of
banality as the wink of Cain. Beside it, thrown in, not folded,
lay a long-abandoned riding coat from London. I was afraid
to lift it out, but my fingers brushed the lapels, satin, dull
with time, and the stock that had been thrust into the pocket
so long ago was once white silk that had turned yellow.

I did lift the fur a few inches, and saw letters, thrown
in with tickets, brochures for cruises long since taken in
boats long since sunk or beached like Dearie, and thrust
among them, abandoned too, a photograph I had already
seen with my mind's eye. There they sat, the women, at a
sidewalk table at the Café de la Paix. Dearie was recogniz-
able; she looked about forty, small, and still slim and pretty
in an almost childish way, sitting a little too close to a woman,
as if she were tethered to her chair.

The woman had what my mother called presence. She
looked large and famous, like women novelists or opera
singers looked then. She was older than the others, who
were leaning toward her at the table. She wore an unfash-
ionable but elegant costume that looked like it had been
made by Worth about 1924, a large hat, Parma violets at her
shoulder, and the inevitable fur piece. She had turned to
say something to a younger woman on her right, a woman
in a frail Chanel suit, with a cloche hat. Nobody was looking
at the camera except Dearie, without a hat, her sleek black
hair cut like Louise Brooks's, staring startled at what must

have been one of those street photographers who still haunt the Place de l'Opéra.

There was nothing so mundane in Dearie's trunk as an ashtray with franc charges on it, but the Paris of the late twenties and the early thirties, with its rich, handsome women of another world, strode out of it, owning the earth for a little while in one city long past, gathering the Dearies of this world in their train. I stroked the fur and thought of her now sparse gray hair, and realized that she, at over seventy, was still tethered as she had been to the woman's chair in Paris, but now it was to her sister, the nearest strong one who would receive and use her, her only protection a tongue soaked in gin. I thought I ought to cry for her, apologize for a secret understanding where there was none, and knew she would call that, in a phrase picked up from her travels, utter bosh.

The phone rang again and again, echoed through the empty halls, bounced against the walls of the empty bedrooms and the living room below me, ringing in a time so far from Paris. It made me stop, afraid to move or even close the trunk until whoever was so insistent somewhere in space had given up. It took a long time. Charley had told me I had better not answer the phone.

I closed Dearie's trunk and leaned against it, disappointed. What I knew then I was really looking for hadn't been there. It was a clue to the way Mrs. Bland had chosen to live, as alien to the valley and as formal and convoluted as the ivory dragons of the devil's work ball she turned in her small gnarled hands, the tea at four o'clock in the bone-china Staffordshire cups with the hunting scenes she told me she ordered from London, what she called the "Chinoiserie influence" in the living room, hardly perceptible except to her, something in the studied casualness of her dress, an insouciance that did not suit her small neat Southern figure. I wanted to tear open all the trunks in the attic to find a clue to where it had come from.

The trunk I turned to was full of canceled checks, the second a series of account books, kept in her cramped hand, all the way back to 1920. I moved fast, once bumping my head on the low ceiling and once stopping as still as a rat, listening to an imaginary sound from below. For some reason I wanted to find what I was looking for before the telephone rang again.

I found it in the fifth trunk, or I think I found it. Ever since that afternoon what I saw in that trunk has given me some sense of a ghostly—yes, it was that—influence that had caused Mrs. Bland to change her rules from Botetourt County to vestiges and hints of what she still called a woman of the world.

"We had thought," she had said a week before at the inevitable tea, "that you were a woman of the world." I had translated this to mean, we thought that you had money— no one there ever said the word "rich."

I was almost afraid to touch anything in the trunk for fear of finding what I was looking for—what had made her begin to nudge me away from their lives when she found that I knew no one she had been taught by some mysterious force and reading and royalty-watching was Europe.

But then, I was so blinded by that mixture of fear and yearning my public love was beginning to turn into that I didn't realize at first that she had heard of no one I knew. She judged as a perpetual tourist snob; her references were those I had been avoiding for years, tenuous connections with ladies who knew friends of the aunt of Mrs. Simpson, like Italian ecclesiastical snobs finding their long paths to cardinals close to the Pope. I lifted off protective layers of the *Tatler*, yellow and slightly smoky. At first I thought the trunk was full of theatrical costumes. Some of them were the kind that people used to keep for costume parties—feathers and masks and Victorian dresses, one with a bustle and a waist that had been let out for a twentieth-century body. They smelled of dusty perfume and rotted silk and the dry scent of decay that old clothes have when a trunk is first opened, which escapes into the air almost at once as if it had been imprisoned there.

I knew they were hers by the neat folds, the tissue paper; she saved herself in layers of time, carefully folded and forgotten. She had added to the trunk as fashions were rejected, until it was full, that phase of life already lived, only residues of habit left, the ones that had "taken" like a vaccination.

A harlequin costume lay on top, and folded in it a program. It was sponsored on October 4, 1927, by the then new chapter of the Junior League, the cast and founding members already grown so old in their houses—Oscar Wilde's *The Birthday of the Infanta,* and *Aria da Capo* by Edna St. Vincent Millay: Eleanor Bland, Pierrot. It had been presented by the Canona Players while they were still all right, as she had said to me in one of her oblique criticisms, brought on by almost anything I said by then, although she still clung to the afternoon visits to get her through till the evening. She complained that they never went to the plays anymore, nice people were no longer involved and strangers had taken over, not, she said, like the old days when we began it and we knew everybody.

Then, at last, I found the ghost, hidden for some long-remembered reason under the rest, out of time's sequence. I tumbled it out onto the floor so that it spread over the photographs of Charley's women, a black lace Balenciaga ball gown, a velvet wrap from Lucien Lelong, beaded and fringed short evening dresses, a fortune in twenties clothes, piled glittering on the attic floor, all filmy and rich and unlike the clothes of the women in Dearie's photograph. These were of the Paris of the Ritz, of Longchamp, of the George V and the Bois, the right bank of Paris in all the ways Mrs. Bland would use the word "right," as far from Dearie's city or mine as I was from Mrs. Bland.

At first I thought the clothes were Mrs. Bland's and that there, in the trunks, I had uncovered some secret richness of choice that they had long forgotten. But they weren't her clothes. Mrs. Bland was a small woman, and these dresses were tall and slim and fitted for what used to be called a stunning figure. I opened a beaded bag and found the name of Letitia Carver, and then I looked again at the labels in the clothes, and her name was embroidered there over and over, a woman who had been dead for years, since I was small. I remembered that it had been sudden and that the grownups stopped talking about it when children came into the room or onto the afternoon porch.

I sat back on the floor and let a lace dress sink into my lap. I knew Broker Carver, who people said had been drunk since the '29 Crash, and who had a sister who worked at the library and disapproved of the books I asked for, and a second sister, Mrs. Wilson, who had lived in a house on the hill I could have seen from the attic window, and who had killed herself there because she was lonesome and afraid to move. Kitty Puss, her daughter, had been at Hilton Head at the time. I knew the house on the river the Carvers had bought from my great-aunt after my great-uncle died, where they lived before they built the castle, and after the Crash.

I had passed the castle whenever I rode the train through the New River Gorge. The Carvers had been coal barons in their day, and their baronial hall had been perched between the mountain they thought was a never-ending source of black diamonds and the river that carried them away. I had watched it from the train window, a ruin long since, as romantic as a Rhine castle, its hundred-foot terrace along the river overgrown with vines, and the wind throwing the shadows of the spindly trees that had grown up between the buckled stones. Fortunes were made quickly then, in the Gilded Age, and lost as quickly, and houses like that were built and fell quickly, too.

But I had long since forgotten Letitia Carver, the third sister, who had died when I was ten. She had been the wild one, who had cut a dash through the valley in her white Cadillac, smoking in public and having dinners for a hundred people sent from Washington, D.C., waiters and all, when she deigned, I heard my mother say, to come back from Paris and London (they were always said together).

"She went to a country-club dance with rouge on her nipples," the women whispered in their soft, shocked voices, "and they showed through her chiffon, and she carried a flask right through the middle of Prohibition that everyone could see." I thought it sounded pretty, to show your pink nipples through your chiffon.

"Oh," they said, forgetting you didn't use the word, "you wouldn't believe how rich the Carvers were, and she ran through thousands." They said thousands in those days, in the early thirties, not millions.

Somehow her fashions, her famous extravagances, her

rules and her caprices had been left in Mrs. Bland's care, her grand, glittering clothes in a grave of fashion in the dusty attic. It was not the ghost of a woman but the ghost of money, blinding the awed eyes of little Eleanor Bland when she was young and newly out of Botetourt County that was haunting me. I sat there on the attic floor for so long, and so quietly, the lace dress still in my lap, that the mice or the squirrels began to chew again in the roof behind the rafters.

When I finally moved to put the clothes and the photographs away, I saw that my mother, who had been born too proud and too cynical to be taken in by the barons, who believed in land not coal, a proud Saxon among the Normans, had gone into the house, and the chair was empty, the chair that was "good taste" from some other ghost that haunted her.

Charley came back late, when it was nearly dark and the colors in the garden where I wandered and waited had turned as bright as under water and the red was disappearing from the roses. He was full of sun and Saturday and the drinks he had had after eighteen holes of golf. He glanced at me as if he was surprised that I was still there.

Dinner had been waiting a long time, designed that way with the joy I still clung to, pushing away the knowledge, as I did whenever the dark cloud came, that it was temporary, the vegetables, the rice, the veal in the oven, cooked as I had learned to cook in France.

"Something smells mighty good," he said finally, playing hillbilly, as he and all of the men in the valley did when they drank; it was one step removed from "niggering," but only a step. It had in it the easy friendly contempt they hid from themselves about the people they called "rednecks."

He put on a record and I knew what it would be. It always was on those rare Saturday nights when we were together in his house.

Nothing he said or did was new that night. It had all happened before, but the afternoon in the attic had made me so aware of all his movements, as if they were new to me, that he caught my eyes and said, "What the hell is the matter?"

I said nothing. I said then, "Nothing. When do you want dinner?"

He didn't answer me; there was ease in his body and in the way he moved around the living room and then the library, almost prowling before he settled down in his father's chair, and held the drink I had made him up against what was left of the light. "Color of a copper penny," he said about the bourbon. "You're learning. What is that smell?"

"That smell is Blanquette de Veau," I said to the fireplace. I was tired of the hillbilly. Once, I had cooked as badly as I could, on a Saturday night at my apartment, and he, coming in the same way from golf and bourbon, had said, "Now, that's some real food. Ain't dat delicious!" Food and culture were mixed in his mind and he was defending both against an attack I hadn't made.

"You said you liked it," I told him. I had forgotten that there was nothing individual about those Saturday nights. They were as formal as a Viennese waltz and as habitual and prejudiced as the men in their pickup trucks whose brag he imitated as if he were a small boy who had slipped away from his mamma to play with them.

"Did I?" He made the ice in his glass tinkle to the rhythm of "Bye, Bye, Blackbird."

I didn't "stand" this. I was grateful to be taken for granted. That is how bad it was, and how miraculous. I saw each quiet moment like this as a silent prayer that would mark someplace within him that would never be the same again, a blessing and a free acceptance that he would miss, and want enough to come back to, sometime, when he could, I always added to myself. Sometimes I had a warning dream of him, climbing a hill, and then turning back before the crest.

He sat easy in his father's chair, his body fallen for the bait of home, not of the play home with me, but of everyday, where he was, habit home. I sat where I had seen his mother sit when he was like this, staring at his drink, remembering too much. I saw her smile and say, "I'd rather have him home when he is like this." He, drunk because he was home, not in a web or a prison, but in a knitted skein of comfort and habit, smiled at me, or his mother, or whoever sat in the same chair at the same time, one of the women in the trunk in the attic. It simply didn't matter.

This was not the ease of Friday but the ease of Saturday, when he moved in a kind of waking sleep, as if he had shut off the life that made his eyes shine when he let himself love me, a pitch of awareness he could no longer stand. But the drunkenness always fooled him. It was not that of evasion, although I think he always hoped it would be, but the real drunkard's darkness, face to the window of life, pressed up against it, seeing the same terrible things, night after night.

They tumbled out as if I were only someone to listen to what I had heard before. I had been fooled by these moments of truth and I had thought at first that the truth would make him free, but I had long since realized that the reality he thought he faced inside the drunkenness was not truth but only a different illusion, an illusion that would be forgotten when he was sober. His dream mind was his own attic trunk, full of the obsessions he would have told the next drunk at the all-night bar, and had, many times. He was the opposite of Charlie Chaplin's drunken millionaire in *City Lights*, recognition and love of me as I was when he was sober, a non-recognition of me as anything but the nearest listener when he was drunk.

The phone rang, and rang again. "Let it go," he told me. I hadn't moved. I knew better. "It's only my goddamn sister-in-law," as if I didn't know Sadie's name and wasn't being as steadily hexed by her as if she had a wax image of me stuck with pins in her dresser drawer under whatever saddle soap she used on her face.

"She's in love with me, like you are," he said. I had heard that before, too, and it was as formal as a wedding. "Thank God, there's no sex between us." I could have chanted that line along with him, part of his litany. He was still for a long time and I hoped that he would not turn on me. He had before, and would again, but for just that minute on just that night, I hoped still to salvage at least the illusion that we were together and not simply in the same room.

He wouldn't eat. Like his mother must have done a thousand times, I tried to get him to eat a little, just a little. I could hear my voice and someone else's and anybody's, all the chorus of women who think they can change things and have fallen in love with lushes, not that solemn word "alcoholics." No, this was a Saturday-night drunk and it was the same as the boy up the hollow who got his pint and took it out to the woods, where the women wouldn't get at him. The only difference was that Charley's woods were in his own living room, not mine, not ever mine and never would be. Like all the other women who have waited like that, I tried not to cry.

Something of where he was came through the self-accusation and family demands, and he looked at me. "You knew I was like this," he said, and then: "They wanted me to marry money. I was raised for that. Father said it was the only hope. She won't let me have you," he said simply, pure fact without comment. I could see him then, huddled with the other men at race meets, at all the accepted sports, the accepted islands, the accepted clubs, men whose wives "had money," a lot of it, all of them held together by that, like veterans of some war where they had been defeated, in cashmere sports jackets they had been given for Christmas.

It shocked me, not because I hadn't seen that market value branded on us, but because it was women who carried that brand, not men. It was part of what I had run away from.

"She crippled me. You see," he said quietly, "she needed a cripple to look after and need her. She wasn't alive without that. She was adrift. Now she has me. You thought I didn't know that. Oh, God, it isn't not knowing. That's where you are such a damned fool.

"Father saw what was happening. He took me abroad once to get me away. I fucked the stewardess the first night we were out at sea on the *Berengaria*."

"Do you remember Letitia Carver?" I asked him. The *Berengaria* had reminded me, and I hoped it would remind him. It was after dinner and he had eaten a little without trouble, and I had sat there watching him. We had gone back into the living room and I was still trying to pretend in the shambles of the evening that I belonged there.

He laughed and he said, "Oh yes, Aunt Letitia. She wasn't my aunt, but I was taught to call her that. Father said Mother and Aunt Letitia looked like Mutt and Jeff."

"Things changed," he said later. "Supper became dinner. Daddy became Father and Mamma became Mother and we weren't allowed to say ma'am anymore like our friends did. Say ma'am, she told us, only to the queen. Father said she was one of those rich snob women who got everything right and yet all wrong. Mother made us drop some of our friends. She called it weeding the garden. I have friends now all over town she's never heard of," he bragged to me, who knew them all in our other life below the hill.

He was quiet for a long time and the late evening came down and filled the living room and I was afraid to move for fear I would stop him saying more. "Money makes the mare go," he said finally. "I don't think she would let me marry anybody but someone with money who looked like Letitia Carver." He no longer cared that it was I who listened. He had a listener. Truth seeped from his mouth, to be forgotten as soon as it was said.

"I threw a present she brought me from Italy down the john." He was gone, sitting there still, but someplace else, someplace that lined his face and silenced him.

He said nothing more until it was time to go to bed, and then he got up, moving like an old man. He said, "Come on. I guess you're going to stay," as if he had been someplace else all weekend, not with me. I lay beside him in the same room that night, untouched and forgotten, more alone than I have ever been in my life.

In the morning, after we had breakfast, I cleaned the kitchen of all clues to me, as if I had committed a murder there.

Charley Bland

At ten o'clock a car drove fast into the driveway. Charley said, "My God, it's Mother," and he ran to the door. I could hear them. "Darling, I rang and rang yesterday. I just had a feeling you needed me. I don't know why. You know I feel things."

He brought her suitcase in and she stopped when she saw me. I had already learned to add to the thick safe tissue of lies that sustained us.

"I just came up to borrow a book," I told her, not even willing her to believe me anymore.

"What book?" She stood in the middle of the bare floor and watched me, preoccupied, a sweet look left over from seeing Charley, and maybe from the praying she had done. I said the first thing that came into my mind, a book I thought she would like. "*Loving*, by Henry Green."

"We don't read books like that," she said, and turned to go upstairs. "Oh," she said in the hall, "I'm so relieved that you're all right. You better see her to her car. I'm so tired after that drive. I got up at dawn."

He leaned into the window of my car. "I'll bring your stuff down to work in the morning." My stuff was the careful gathering of gown and scent and robe and all those things that were meant to please him. I could see them, stuffed into a corner of his closet so she wouldn't find them before he had a chance to spirit them out to his car, and I could see myself stuffed there, too, in the dark, and my picture in the trunk along with the others. I drove away, too used to all of it by then even to cry. You don't cry in nightmares, or react, and you know better than to run; you know it won't do any good. They just happen and you get through them.

One More River

That summer, when Charley Bland could find an excuse to be away for whole days and nights without Sadie and Cuddy wanting to come too, we went to the river, to a fishing camp he had shared for years with Plain George, where nobody had fished for a long time. Sometimes Plain George went with us, that benign man. It was a haven for both of them, hidden from the demands of Mrs. Bland and Sadie and Anne Randolph. I remember these escapes as one night, a night of rain and quiet and steady drinking, when Charley had lied his way to the river and Anne Randolph had gone to New York.

All that night we sat on the screened porch by the river and listened to the rain fall on the water. They had passed through drunkenness to the dream of clarity on the other side that drinkers seek and seldom find, the place of peace where everything is possible and clean, and there is no danger, no denial, no no, and you can do anything, anytime, drive anywhere at any speed, and the future will be different and possible, and there are usually, for Southern men, no women.

Women, to them, are dictators or servants. The souls of dead slaves have crept into their habits to haunt them, and they learn only two ways to live, obey or rebel, or, as we did that night, all those nights, escape, lie, hide, and comfort each other.

We listened to the rain on the tin roof that early morning, for the birds were beginning their dawn cry, even in the darkness and the rain, on the screened porch, in the silence, the ice long since used up. It was still black dark outside, but we knew the river was there, we could hear it as the rain fell steady on the water, then changed rhythm as the wind slewed it across the surface, a counterpoint to the rain on the roof.

The two of them, best friends, had sat on this screened porch year after year, in the one place where it seemed that things never changed, with these glasses, in the once dark-green wicker porch chairs that had long been rejected when the porches disappeared from the "restored" houses. The chairs had been old when they were brought out to the fishing camp. In the years of neglect they had become dirt-colored and sprung and flattened and easy.

No time passed. We listened to the rain while they drank, and spacious with fatigue, I rested in love, in the same timeless and peaceful illusion. If the place was haunted, it was haunted with the smell of old damp, and the marks of all the bodies in all the years of sitting so, and lying so, on the bare bed where the tin roof had leaked and darkened the mattress in streaks that looked like someone had been crying, or semen had stained it or the vaginal gifts of all the women who had loved there when it was dark that way in all the nights as the rain came down on the roof and the river and there was no time. Drink and love had taken time away so often there that they were used to it, the two best friends.

It stopped raining and the wind died just before dawn. The sky was alive with birdsong, and a little morning breeze shivered the wet leaves and touched my face. It was late June and the dawn came at its earliest when the world was asleep except for the birds, and people who had sat all night in the patience of love or drink with no time passing.

Charley got up slowly, as he, or Plain George, had all night long, and took the glasses into the lean-to kitchen they wouldn't let me clean. It was one of the thousand versions of Bobby Low's "You can go if you'll keep up," an almost formal series of gestures, of dancing to their tune, that meant I could stay.

Charley came back from the kitchen. "We've run out."

Plain George leaned down to take his socks off. "The river's too high for the car. All this rain," he told Charley.

I looked out. The dawn had come faintly, so that I could see that the river ran yellow and curled over the ford we had crossed. The water would have come up over the floor of Plain George's Porsche. It was running fast in the first swell after the rain, before the morning slowed its pace again and we could drive across.

Both of the men rolled their pant legs high and slung their shoes around their necks by the laces. "Are you coming?" Charley said; he had not explained where.

Plain George, always a little more thoughtful at such times, added, "You'd better come. You won't see this often."

There were times when he seemed born to pick up after Charley. His was the extra smile to smooth indifference, the visit to the lawyer when the car had been wrecked, and, in the past, the call to the girl's parents to apologize and lie. He was doomed to kindness.

He had married Anne Randolph while she was still fat, a deep act of compassion she had never quite forgiven. She still watched him like a hawk. It did no good. He had been visiting Sigsbie, who "did" all the ladies' nails, including Anne Randolph's, every Thursday evening and every Monday afternoon for nearly twenty years, leading two lives as easily as most men lead one. His friends left messages for him at Sigsbie's apartment.

Charley waded first into the swollen water. It came up to his hips. Nobody mentioned that it was at floodtide. Neither did I. It was one of the rules about keeping up.

We crossed where the river was a hundred feet wide. There had once been a dam, sunk and silted up years ago into a ford. The dawn damp clung to my face and I wanted to wipe it from my eyes, but I dared not lose balance. It felt like tears.

They twisted and danced in the water ahead of me as if they were trying to free themselves from the wild current. Once Plain George stumbled and recovered. Charley went steadily, delicately, finding smooth rocks with his feet, which seemed to have sight of their own. I tried to follow his footsteps, as I had for a long time. No one looked back.

The river tugged and tore at my clothes. The river rocks were too sharp or too slick. The rushing water was up to their hips, up to my waist, clinging, heavy, viscous yellow water. I tried to dodge branches, bits of trash wood, and once, a drowned water rat carried along the high humped back of the river lodged for a second against my arm and then swung away downriver again before I could shake it off.

They were walking up the other side, their clothes dripping. The CANONA COUNTRY CLUB on the back of Charley's old tennis shirt had turned from green to a brackish black. Plain George's Brooks Brothers shirt had escaped from his pants and clung to his broad beam, which made me feel safer than I was, more comforted than anyone intended.

They intended nothing but getting across the river. Behind them I was a drummer boy, a soldier, a pioneer, a dog. I struggled up the bank and let down my skirt that I had tied around my waist. It hadn't helped. The soaked skirt slapped against my legs. They went on walking barefooted down the path beside the rain-soaked country road, deep in black river-bottom mud from the night. The soft grass and the patches of mud felt good between my toes, child feet again. We stooped where the water oaks and the willows bent down to the water, and the rain from the branches cascaded down our backs.

Slowly, softly, we all began to take the pace of the dawn, forget the struggle with the water in the new cold beginning of the morning. My senses were stretched and humming like wires from fatigue. We walked for half an hour and no one said a word. They went as if this path along the river were a place that they came to for a peace even more timeless than the peace they found at the fishing camp.

The river was already going down. I could tell by the branches that I could see floating by, slower now, under the dawn mist that was rising from the water. The fish were beginning to feed; they made little bubbles on the yellow surface. Here and there dragonflies hovered, and once I heard a heavy plop of some animal diving into the water from someplace hidden in the bank. It was quiet and gentle and smelled of rain and green growth and wet earth.

The ramshackle ghost of what had once been a pretty cottage lay in the mist across the water. Its roof had been patched a long time ago with tar paper that made a quilt of different-colored squares. The ghost of what had been a wide porch sagged toward the ground, brought down by the ghost of a tree that had grown into the end of it. On the porch there was even the shape of a swing.

Someone sometime had painted the walls. The board and batten siding were not raw wood, but had been left to streak with a faint reminder of white paint. I could see that long ago the fruit trees in the meadow had been white-washed, as people used to do to keep the insects from the fruit, but there were only hints of gray trunks from across the river. That was all I could see, a place that had gone to seed, become again its raw materials behind the morning mist, where the human marks of care were only hints of work long finished, the people long lost, the house delicate again, fallen, deserted. Sometime there had been a lawn, but it had long since turned into deep meadow. The grass and weeds were veiled silver with dew or the last of the rain.

Charley stood on the bank, looking taller in the first light than he was. He cupped his hands around his mouth and called, "Set us over!" In the first light of the morning, "Set us over!" sounded ghostly too, in the mist that caught it and flung it as a whisper in the air. He called again, "Set us over!" louder, more insistent, a slow, haunted, ancient call. He and Plain George watched quietly then, their shoes still slung around their necks. They had caught the patience of the morning and the place, fallen, neglected patience. Finally the shadow of a door opened on the porch, and someone came out. Only his size told me it was a man, that and his long country stride across the wet meadow. He looked angled and weightless. He disappeared behind the willows grown down the bank, and reappeared, a stick figure in that light, on a frail jetty, like a line drawing smudged with mist.

We waited, far upriver, and no one said a word. The morning breeze made me shiver, and something else, a sense of being in a deserted world, where no one knew where we were or cared, all lines cut, as if we were lost creatures, having only each other.

Gradually the hollow sound of oars came nearer as a johnboat grew larger out of the mist. The boatman had gauged exactly how far upriver he had to row on that morning in that current to reach where we stood on the opposite bank. He and Charley together had charted the flow of the river.

We got into the boat. Only the boatman reached up to help me in, some good manners left from a long time ago that would not let him show surprise that a woman was there. He muttered, "Howdee, ma'am," low in his throat, as if he had not spoken aloud for a long time. I sat huddled in the prow, and the current took us in a long line across and down the river. It was cold.

They talked almost in whispers, or the current was too noisy for me to hear what they were saying, or to pay attention. They seemed to have known each other for a long time in a past I had not been a part of. I think that I didn't pay attention because I was so intent on the house that was coming nearer and nearer and defining itself in the mist.

The boatman nudged into the slatted jetty without wasting an oar stroke.

Just as we docked, the sun broke through and made the meadow shimmer. Our weight and the current shivered the water-rotted slats under us as we walked up to the bank. I looked down at the river flowing below my feet and was afraid of falling. It was only when we got to the bank that I was able to look up and see where I was.

The tree at the end of the porch was hidden in a huge wisteria vine, heavy with bloom, that had long since killed it. The vine was slowly, patiently, taking the porch down. It had crawled along the roof and had begun to finger a broken dormer window.

Men seemed to have fallen where they were when sleep came, and they were getting up and disappearing into the underbrush that grew all around the meadow. One nodded shyly over his shoulder, a hint of hospitality left as the streaks of white paint were left on the house. One had been under an elder tree, one in the swing, and inside the house, through the door that the boatman hadn't bothered to close, I could hear men moving. They moved as animals would move in a lair, slowly, stretching, coming closer to stare and sniff at us.

There were six or seven men there. I couldn't count. One kept pacing back and forth at the rear, and I thought I counted him twice, three times. I couldn't tell. They seemed to be of an age, and then I could see that they must have ranged from about fifteen, a boy who was pacing and staring as if he had never seen a woman before, to the oldest, the boatman with tufts of gray at his temples and a face lined, not so much with age as with weather. There was a growl of waking behind the door when we were ushered in, and he called to whoever it was, "We got company."

"Hey, Seth"—of course, they would all have had names like Seth, left over from their Pentecostal births. "Git up, we got company. This here's Seth; he's our cousin," he explained to Charley, not to me, not to Plain George. These were Charley's friends, the kind of friends he had made, in a map of people all over the valley and the hills behind it in his vast flirtation with freedom, the lost, the feral, the unknown, as far from the other polite life he lived as we were far from whatever we called home.

Seth, who lay on the bed, was a stranger to him. "How do." Charley dropped into hillbilly talk as if it were another language.

"You set down," the boatman said, remembering me, and I sat as he told me to, in an old rocker where the arms had long since been worn smooth by whoever had sat in it, grown old in it. The room was nearly dark; it had been a dog-run hall, but it had been made into a bedroom, if having a bed in a corner of it could make it any function except shelter. It smelled sick-animal bad, but the bad was old, too, as if something had died in there and had already dried up before anybody bothered to get rid of it.

Seth had one leg. He had roused himself up to be polite, and he half lay, half leaned, as a concession to company, on the surface of a bed where the quilts had so long since lost their color that it took time to see that they were quilts at all, and then I saw that one had been made in a wedding-ring pattern, maybe red and green, like my aunt used to make. It took her all winter, in the evenings.

It was a dog bed that had been slept on, risen from,

slept on again, without any of the luxuries of sheets, of even smoothing it. It could have been covered with straw like a surface in a den.

He lay behind one large gray foot that from where I sat dominated the bed; he was so tall his face seemed far away behind it. He didn't take his eyes off me. He had a shotgun beside him, and his hand hovered over it. He looked scared. He was poised there, as wary as an animal, struggling with waking up, with fear, and with politeness.

"Oh hell, Seth, excuse me, ma'am, put that thing away; it ain't nobody but Charley from upriver."

"Howdee," Seth said, the word and accent of an eighteenth-century English duke. "Howdee, ma'am," he said again, this time to me. He put his hands together in his lap, being nice to company at six o'clock in the morning. The boy had flung open the rear door and was standing in it to hear what was going on. He had edged nearer and nearer to me, as you would edge toward a wild thing so as not to frighten it until you got near enough to touch it.

The new sun flooded in and lit linoleum that had been yellow and brown. It touched the pictures of John L. Lewis and Mother Jones and Jesus with the lantern knocking at a garden gate far far away from Ford Madox Brown, who had painted it in England a long time ago.

Somehow, like an altar, the mantel over the trash-clogged fireplace had been left or forgotten from when someone had put there a single china candlestick, a postcard that had gilt on it, a baby shoe, and one of those big palmetto fans with a painted poinsettia that people used to bring back from Florida.

I could see the other men way at the back of the house, watching, not saying a word, a little pack of them under the gnarled tree where the apples had lain so long the year before that the tree hovered over its own seedlings. Three yellow hounds looked up at the sound of the voices inside the house, stretched, and went to sleep again.

"Seth thought you was the sheriff." The boatman apologized for his cousin's lapse of manners with the gun. "He don't like the sheriff. He's our cousin and we ain't goin to let nobody have him."

Charley seemed to be understanding between the lines what the boatman was saying.

"They ain't gone come for me. What the hell, excuse me, ma'am, would I do in the county jail like this? I got me a leg give to me by the army but the damn thing hurts, excuse me, ma'am," Seth was saying. "I don't want to go. I just don't want to. Hit wudn't my fault no how. He made me do it."

Charley looked at the boatman, whose name nobody ever told me. The boatman said, "He had to kill a man, but hit wudn't his fault. His mamma sent him up here to us'n. We ain't goin to let nobody have him."

They looked at me, and I, who was beginning to understand the unspoken language of men about to talk more important business than murder and mamma, but not in front of a woman, went out and sat on the back porch steps and watched the meadow and tried not to stare at the men, who had begun to hunker down under the tree, looking at me as if I were some alien thing, interesting but not of the world, that had wandered there to their back stoop. They had the I-seen-plenty-of-them look of hillbillies at their first carnival.

I could hear what they were saying in the room behind me, but only in fragments; voices low and rumbling in their throats as men's voices are when they take each other for granted.

"I got to use the commode. Look and see there ain't nobody acrost the river," Seth said. I could hear the creak of the bed as he got up. "Hell no, I ain't goin out thar with her." I could hear a crutch hit the floor and the sound of foot and crutch as he disappeared off the front porch.

There were more murmurs, and the boatman said, "How much you want?" and then, sometime later, "Hell no, we don't do nuthin. We all got rocking-chair money from Korea. I could tell you things." But he didn't. There was a long silence. I heard, "I don't know. You remember what a pretty place this was, Charley? Mamma died and thar wudn't nobody to do nuthin."

The silence after that sounded comfortable, as if they were prepared to just sit wherever they had lit and be in the same place for a while. "Seth? He got the pension for his leg and he got the Silver Star."

Somebody asked a question I didn't hear, and then the end of something: "That's what he done. He didn't know no better." What seemed a long time later: "Oh, I don't know. Mamma died while we's all gone and when we come back we didn't have to do nuthin, with the rocking-chair money and the vederans . . . They ain't a man out thar didn't go. We all went together. We got three Bronze Stars and fourteen Purple Hearts and one Silver Star between us."

"Oh hell, it don't mean nuthin," he said after another long, comfortable pause, and then, "Wudn't that a good rain?"

I could hear Seth coming back along the porch, the thud of his bare foot, then the sharp hit of the crutch. I began to count them, thud hit thud hit. They stopped. The bed creaked as he lay down on it again.

The boy had crept closer and he stood a few feet from me, just looking, what Charley would have called peekin and peerin. One of the men behind him called out, but a call that was a whisper anywhere else in the world. "Ain't you never saw a woman before, Little Dudley?" I had been mistaken. Not only the Bible, but last name first, family names, too, pedigrees carried on their backs.

I watched the grass at my feet. I reached down and picked a blade and smoothed it in my hand.

"You know how to whistle through them things?" Little Dudley's voice sounded rusty.

He watched my mouth, waiting for it to open. I was afraid to say anything, but he waited until I finally said, "Can you?"

"Here." He sat down close to me. "Here, lemme show you." He put a blade of grass between his thumbs and lifted it to his lips and blew a shrill whistle, reverberating the grass blade like a reed.

I tried it. Nothing happened. I could sense the men, who were drawing a little nearer. I blew again and there was a faint sound.

"That one ain't no good. Take and use this here one." Little Dudley handed me a wider blade of grass, and held my hands to put it straight between my thumbs.

I blew. There was a shrill whistle. One of the men said, "Now, wudn't that good? Wudn't that good?" He had turned to the others. Somebody at the back said yes, that was real good.

Charley had come out onto the stoop behind us at the

sound of the whistle. "We're leaving," he said. He didn't ask about the whistle.

I don't remember being in the boat again, or how we got back into town, or even if Mrs. Bland or Sadie or Anne Randolph found out where we had been. I think Sadie did. I have a vague picture of her standing by the car, that time or another time. That time or another time we had dropped off the edge of our world and somehow we always came back.

But sometimes I sleep too deeply, and when I wake up, there is no memory of a dream. I only know that I am going there again to a forever lair of men without women, and a voice cries, "Set us over!" across one more river. There, in the dream or in the lost time, I have found something and escaped something. Nothing dies. It only becomes timeless.

True Pitch

In the Tarot pack there is one unnumbered card. It is the Fool, who whirls at the center of things but is outside the movement of the other cards. He wears, of course, a coat of many colors, red for celestial fire, blue for purity, yellow for joy. The bag on the end of the staff he carries is light— but it has in it the burden of his mind. He is being bitten on the left ankle by a white lynx. The left is his unconscious side, what is left of his remorse, his lucidity; but he does not see this.

He goes on, fool that he is, toward a crocodile which is ready to devour him and return him to chaos. He could be saved by his heavenly gold belt, by the flower that grows at his feet, but impulse carries him on, whirling, timeless, joyful fool, pure balance, clown, heaven and earth, scapegoat and ritual sacrifice. Because he is at the center of things, and outside at the same time, he is pure balance, invisible.

His movements are felt only as the slight wind on a cheek, on a hand, that makes a person smile, not knowing why.

It is the seventh sense, the sense of balance. There is no word for it. Athletes know it, when in golf, in the split second of the back swing, they know that the drive will be perfect, in some pure arc within the two edges of fault. Tennis players know it when, in the second's pause, remembered as it lingered there in air, the racket meets the thrown ball and they know they are going to ace. It is sensed, hardly registered, simply lived. In music it is called true pitch. We had it for a few months that first summer.

Love was the Fool at the center of things, poised there, not hidden, but invisible. There was within that summer a place of balance between things as they were and things as they might be, between public and private love, between demands and wishes, between opening up to a company that came up the hill and along the back of a mountain ridge and the silence and peace of being alone. It lasted only for a little while. Now remembered, as that second of pure balance is remembered, it seems to have lasted a long time.

It was a time of evenings and afternoons, and even as late as the last star watched lowering on the last of night before Charley Bland went down the hill and along the five miles of the hollow road, drawn into his parents' house to wake up there in the morning.

I rented an 1830 cabin that summer. My mother helped me furnish it. She found she could spare some of the early-American furniture she had collected for years for the colonial kitchen she had made in the basement. It was right for the cabin, and well worth the sacrifice, she said, so I could work again. What she meant was that she was glad to get me out of the house, to move the center of my happiness and the waves it caused out of her sight. She and my father had wanted me to be there, at home when they needed me, but not underfoot, and they were already tired of waiting for something to happen.

My mother was an impatient woman. She saw, long before I did, that things were settling back to the level they had always been. I had been like a spring freshet, but now it was July, slow and indolent, too hot for anyone to care or even judge. We were simply being forgotten for a while, let live.

The cabin was in the mountains between the outermost green of the new golf course of the new country club and the lost and hidden hollows where my neighbors were as wary as the squirrels they hunted.

There, between the hillbilly haunters and the owners who drove their golf carts over the ridges and the high valleys that had once been as unknown as my neighbors, I found my place. It was a year of unemployment in the state so bad that it would help John Kennedy to the Presidency, but the primaries were over, and my silent furious neighbors were already being forgotten again.

There were virgin logs nearly forty feet long above the two doors that entered into what had been two rooms and now was one. They were the measure and the strength of the cabin, which had been there since 1830, when some early family, like the mountaineers down the hollow from me, had come to hide and live and be let alone. So had I and so had Charley Bland.

Inside the long room, like a huge primitive altar, was an eight-foot-square fireplace of mud and stone that had heated both rooms. Sometimes at night we would lie and stare at it until, like clouds or the faces in the wood of

Sadie's living room, the old men would come out of the stones to watch us. I still see them, too, trailing long mud beards, the profiles of old rabbis, the eyes of stone.

The walls were covered with a plaster made of lime from the burning of the bones found in the ancient graves of the mound builders, fine creek-bottom sand, and water. It was as hard as rock, uncracked in all that time. The weather had streaked it through the years where the hard rain had flung itself past the overhanging eaves.

I had my dog, Jubal, there, young that year and boundless in pursuit of phantoms only he saw across the high fields. Sometimes, toward the fall, when he could get her away, Charley brought his setter, Birdy, and we ran them in the old neglected farmlands beyond the golf course, where, like my neighbors, the coveys from the lost cornfields that were now fairways had hidden.

A seven-foot black snake lived under the back stoop and kept the mice away. I left milk for it in a saucer. It had been there, after all, longer than I had. I think the balance began to tip for me first, just a hint of our future fall, when I came home one day to find two mountain neighbors proudly holding its lithe rope of a body on a branch.

"We killed it fer ye, lady," they said, pleased to take care of their neighbor, who was there so much alone.

On Saturdays and Sundays, after the men played golf, after the children were hauled out of the pool, the friends we made together came along the ridge and the station wagons gathered and we sat as alike as crows along the front stoop, with our legs hanging over, dressed that year in Bermuda shorts and bleeding Madras shirts, told stories, played, and shared salad and bourbon and the pleasing sense that we all belonged there with Charley Bland.

They were younger than we were. In that place, as formal as a tribal group, age mattered. There were still "age groups" long since established. Ages mixed at large parties, not at small ones, so that Sadie's subtribe and the remnants of Charley Bland's "sacred circle" were older, and Sadie's social dictatorship stopped at some magic barrier. She fumed all summer at the edge of it.

Sometimes she and whatever friend she was teaching to ride would hack up the back hollow roads from the stable, two miles away, and tether there long enough to have a drink, a stirrup cup, Sadie called it, sitting her horse above us, refusing to dismount.

So, until they were forced later either to defend me or drop me, a choice that turns friendship into partisanship and destroys its delicacy, we gathered there, in the sun, in the afternoons, in the high summer days.

Charley Bland was happy that summer, almost silly with it, not glimpsed, not turned away, for the first time since anyone remembered, but basking, unprotected. That look of joy, the laughter, was not fleeting, evocative, as it had been so long, but fully there, unafraid that something would be taken from him.

The balance between us was physical, too. One day he stood below the back stoop, which was built up five feet above the ground, with one of those crossed lattices below it that made a storage space, and a home for my black snake. He braced his foot against the lattice and held up his hand, and I took it and pitched him up onto the porch without weight, without thought. One of the men said, "I didn't see that." But he had.

Sometimes I would feel a shadow and want to warn him. He would stretch his legs from the old rocking chair

I had found and put on the front porch, all the way to the edge of the floor, where his feet could touch the heads of the summer flowers I had planted there, and look so content that he took my heart. It was like those times when you know you have to wake someone but let them sleep a little longer, because in the depths of their dreams they look like the angels that stories say they were once, before their earthly life. That look, as fleeting as the moment of true pitch, was a blessing for him, and I would not have dared wake him.

Years later, after the destruction of that summer, I wrote a story and I put Jake Catlett and his family there, in my cabin, the only house in the county that I remember as truly mine, that I shared for a little time with Charley Bland and my friends, but for longer, so much longer, with those who had built it, come before me, before there were country clubs and forgotten people hidden in their quiet fury that summer in the hollows below me.

Now Jake Catlett, father and son, and Essie, vast and ponderous, sitting there in a September fiction, are more real to me than the station wagons that were parked along the dirt road on Sunday afternoons, in the few months of the cabin's long life when it was a haven for us and an amusement for a summer.

That was what it was that year. I can see, still, Charley treating it as if it were his home, as hospitable as the ancestor of the house who might have welcomed travelers the same way, thirsting for company and for news.

People who have fallen from heights and lived have told about a moment when they seem to pause, and there is the illusion that the air is holding them up and letting them drift as safe as feathers. That's the way it was, for all of us, Charley, our friends that were not his friends or my friends, but whom, for a little while, we shared.

Then, one late Sunday afternoon, when they had all gone away, Charley stayed a while, as he usually did. We fell asleep on the wide couch bed on the side of the cabin I had made into a living room.

We woke up as if we had been drenched with ice. Sadie, looking as dangerous as a Hun invader, was sitting above us on her horse, staring into the window as if she wanted to tear the cabin down, log by log.

What Sadie and Mrs. Bland said to Charley I never knew, but there was a weather change. After that I was alone a lot there, and when I went into the town to the perpetual parties that had long since replaced the church, the quilting bees, the fall hunts of all our grandparents, I came back alone.

One night I was caught in an early deep snow that came to the mountains in the fall, and my car ran into a snowbank and I had to walk a mile through it in my stockings because my party shoes gave out almost at once. After I got home I lit the fire and danced with its leaping shadows all alone in the night, to a twenties record Charley Bland had brought me.

"Charleston, Charleston," "I Can't Give You Anything but Love," Voh doh do-de-oh doh doh do-de-oh doh, "Yes! We Have No Bo-Nan-Os"—I danced to them all in the night, before the fire that flung its light, touching the walls around the darkened room, making my shadow surge and dip. I danced with my own shadow, like the whirling Fool, until the spirit came back into my frozen legs and, for a little while, I warmed into the most pure happiness I ever had there.

Fall into Winter

That was in the fall, when the charmed summer of welcome and tea and balance had ended.

As October passed, and the leaves turned, and the fire was lit in the Blands' living room, the scene there changed. Mrs. Bland had let me know that the afternoons were over. She thanked me and said they had gotten her through the summer, which had always bored her, now that she couldn't swim anymore. But when September came, she explained, there were meetings to go to, the committees she sat on, her church work, all that, and her afternoons were taken up.

At Mr. Bland's command, she asked me, twice a week, formally, to come for "drinks" and dinner, so that I would know that I was a part of those days, and those days only. She would ask me to be there when Mr. Bland came home.

"Mr. Bland"—she called him that to me always; somewhere in her past, which went back so far into fears I did not know, women referred to their husbands by their last names to callers, and I was a perpetual caller. "You are," she said, "good for him. There are things you have in common that bore me stiff."

He sat in the same chair by the window where she sat in the afternoons, and his props were there, too, waiting for him, prepared: the *Times* refolded, the cushions shaken. The same silver tray was brought in by Randolph, who changed his coat for evening after he raked the leaves and burned them, so that the hillside was scented with sweet smoke.

Every evening Mr. Bland asked Charley if he had had a drink or if he wanted one, and Charley, the wild colonial boy, the rake, the devil with the women, would stand "first on one foot and then on the other" and answer that he wanted one. Mr. Bland told Charley his fidgets made him nervous. When he said that, they fell into a blank silence for a while, not of peace, but of being afraid to speak because Mr. Bland was in one of his moods.

So the room changed and remained the same, the prayer rug from Kerman that Dearie had brought back, the chair, the candlesticks on the mantelpiece, the fire in the hearth, and I, embarrassed for Charley, staring at the worn carpet that Mrs. Bland complained about whenever she bothered to look down.

I loved the carpet, with its faint shadows of Arabic writing, the evocation to Allah. It was so worn that the animals were ghosts of gazelles, and lions and rebellious griffins, trapped in what had once been cages of blue and green vines, now as fawn-colored as the pelt of some animal in a sand-swept land. I spent a lot of time that fall looking at the animals in their medallions, and their formal fights, while they scraped the family evening emery board in which I had no part as myself, only as a weapon.

Each of them saw me in a different way, and used what they saw. Mr. Bland had taken to tossing questions at me, like, "What did Meister Eckhardt *mean?*" I had lent him a book he was curious about, and he was, verbally, throwing it back at me.

"Do you think Hamlet was crazy?" He glared at me. I didn't know how to answer. I sensed that the question had nothing to do with a play called *Hamlet*, and I was right. He was as tired of waiting as my parents were. He was demanding action of me and I didn't know what to do.

"She never reads anything worth talking about, and Charley never reads anything at all." He nodded toward Mrs. Bland as if she were not sitting on the sofa with a slight smile left on her face from something she had been thinking. She had long since stopped listening to him.

The dusk came down earlier and earlier into a kind of staged peace, where the valley below and the river changed color and then, by October, were gone altogether and the valley was a floor of lights like fallen stars.

That was the font of our public love, that room with its worn carpet. It was from there that decisions were made, which doors were open, which were shut. Everything else that happened to us spread out from there between five-thirty to bedtime, in the clink of glasses in the silence, a toilet flushing away in the stillness when Dearie heaved herself up and wandered off to bed, the gibes, the habits, the hours and hours of dinner, sometimes peaceful, more often full of obstacles of silence, with Sadie staring at me from across the late-fall asters on the white tablecloth, preoccupied with her obsessive hatred. But she could not yet do anything about it, not at those holy hours anyway. They were the times the family had to be together at all costs.

The cost was high. Tolstoy defined boredom as the desire for desire, but what he did not face was more terrible. The desire for boredom is stronger. It is dangerous to disturb it. I was beginning to find out, in my own preoccupation, in time, in diminishment, how high the cost was.

I had broken their rules, not by a love affair with Charley—his love affairs amused them for a while, and always had—but by trying to live there, and even to be happy, when I had been cast as a visitor. There was no room for me in their habits.

They had seemed curious for a while about whatever it was my legend convinced them that I cared about. I found myself, out of love for Charley Bland, discussing Mrs. Bland's mild, well-written domestic books I never would have read, and attitudes I had long forgotten that the ladies on the hill took for granted.

But gradually, like Kierkegaard's tame geese, they grew tired of me, and the love that had brought me home retreated into secrecy. In public, the old habits of being the family bachelor and the extra man for their gentilities took over Charley Bland, and I, who had already said all that they were interested in, was beginning to be put aside, not even unkindly—that would have had emotion in it—but like a book they had read. I had mistaken their habit of hospitality for affection; it was, in me, a grievous fault.

Charley's mother even explained it. She said that they never knifed anybody out of malice, only if they got in the way. It was the clearest definition of psychopathic reasoning I had ever heard. So the decision to ignore my existence was not malicious, except for the women led by Sadie, who wanted to kill me but didn't know it yet. They simply watched me, still invited me to their parties in deference to Charley for a while, and waited for a sign. I had been so happy that summer that I didn't know how quietly they were waiting.

More often, though, I was having to make way for the new—the new visitor, the new person who had come from someplace else, anyplace, as if they sought the heavens for a new way to fly—so long as the resident weekly wild goose didn't hang around too long.

I had longed for this safe scene, this harshness, this warmth, even this role they cast me in and were growing tired of. Sometimes I had a hint of truth, which I rejected, that I had sold something of my soul for it.

I had succumbed to coming back to live, and the first fine days of what Mr. Bland called "the prodigal" were over. The meat had grown cold, the cost was being added, and they who looked forward to my coming, day after day, had grown bored. There was something they missed, and Charley thought, and both our mothers, bored and isolated, too, thought, I would bring it back, but they had heard all that, and it wasn't much, after all, just people they didn't know and books they never wanted to read.

I was gradually becoming to them a non-person, like a Russian poet living in some faraway cold city with no library and no one to talk to. In the beginning it was a relief.

So, in order to placate, the way he had done all his life, Charley became charming again in public, alone, and we lived our life in private. He came less and less to the cabin in the earlier darkness of fall.

We began to seek, not to be accepted any longer, but

only to be allowed to live day by day, and it was granted to us by bartenders, waiters, people we made quick anonymous friends with in the slow time of night in the animal clubs—the Elks, the Moose, the Bear, safer than the Wayfaring Stranger, where public and private love met too often. I knew him in the valley, where we found a new secrecy, a series of retreats from the rigid social lives in the small hills above the city, and a new life in places they either did not know or rejected—the bars, the Greasy Elbows, the truckers' motels. It opened by accident a whole life for me that as a member of that narrow country-club world I would never have known—a gift they never meant to make me.

Mr. Bland was right, though. Like and love didn't have a damn thing to do with each other. Of all of them, Charley as well, I liked Sadie best. She had been knocking at the same door that was being shut to me for fifteen years, trying to get in. If there were parts for bachelor uncles to play, and for maiden aunts, there was also the accepted treatment of in-laws.

She was the butt of too many jokes. She had been left out of decisions too often, and she had fought all of this with a passion that had been born in her for better things. What they had been she had long since lost sight of, if she ever knew in words; but there had been dreams knocked out of her. They all, by the time I knew her, were vague. She had sacrificed something, and she had almost forgotten what it was. I have always thought of her when I hear the words from *On the Waterfront* quoted as a joke: "I could have been a contender." Far from the waterfront and in a less militantly genteel world, Sadie, too, could have been a contender, for what she didn't know, but she knew with her whole soul that something she didn't and couldn't name was holding her back.

Up to the time I came back it had been something vague that haunted her, hurt her feelings. A letting of blood she didn't dare show at the eternal dinner table made her fight for what she would have called consideration, if she had given a word to what she longed to have from them: attention, affection, even the chance for servitude.

She was simply there, trying her best to be a part of running things, and not to fall back into some shadowed limbo with Dearie, sucking on her gin, where nobody heard what she said at all. She even took the teasing, finally, like the good sport they demanded, and ran Cuddy and the rest of the world as a solace for her ever-present defeat in the house with the worn carpet and the glasses and the gibes, and the constant forgetfulness as soon as she left the room. Of course, when I came back she had an object on which to focus all of whatever it was—not frustration, for that would have implied that someone had bothered to keep her from doing what she wanted—but deadly polite indifference.

I looked at her sometimes, and her face in repose reminded me of a cold, marble bas-relief in the Baths of Diocletian in Rome, a sleeping, beautiful, young, sad, guileless, brutal, brave, terrible Medusa. If the old men in her living room had seen her that way, or she had seen them, she would have painted them over as an intrusion and judgment on a life she planned and had to control every minute of every day.

The fall of the year was Sadie's weapon. Her close friends were home again. They had been scattered through the month of August, from Daisy and Lewis at Martha's Vineyard (not the artistic end, Daisy told me) to Maria at a cottage at Egeria, to Melinda Cutright at Virginia Beach, to Kitty Puss at what she called that goddamned Hilton Head, where her husband, Brandy Baseheart, had insisted on buying what she called a condom.

The weapons of caste and weather and time were all Sadie had. She used them. When the women came inside from the tennis courts and the swimming pools and sending their children off to well-chosen schools around the East Coast, and were gathered like a harvest in the Williamsburg living rooms and often in her own corner of California, she was able to get to work. Because she couldn't influence anything in the citadel living room so long as Mr. Bland held the reins, she ruled the women with a rod of iron.

I became, when the bridge games started and the volunteer meetings, and the "drinks" and "drinks" from evening to evening at each other's houses, Sadie's total obsession. I even had to respect that. It was clean, dangerous, focused, passionate hate.

Fortunately or unfortunately, I was not there to fight it, if I had known how. I don't think it would have mattered, since that kind of profane hate is as hard to judge or contain as profane love, and is its mirror opposite, not a *coup de foudre*, but a sword of ice. I had heard of a man in Germany who had been killed by the fall of a six-foot icicle. Sadie would have done the same had she—not dared, she was brave and would have dared—rather, had she thought of it. I'm sure that waiting for someone to die was, in her case, in the living room at drink time, focused by then entirely on me.

There are two, maybe, having known Sadie, three, timeless places: the place of love, the place of hate, and the place, in my case, of work. That saved me. No matter what was happening to me otherwise, the work was there, more demanding than any rejection, more alive than any public habit. It was sustained, although he never let himself accept that, by the evasive, dear, almost secret love of Charley Bland, a secrecy he railed against as an intrusion, pacing the floor of the cabin, blaming me, bringing friends there, all men, to drink while I read Kierkegaard's *Concluding Unscientific Postscript* in the bathroom.

Sadie at the same time went to play bridge, and what mountain people call "hating me out" was planned over a bridge table at Daisy's. I could see her blue-green living room with the fire lit, and the drinks at ten o'clock in the morning, and the cards sliding professionally around the table, and the sounds of a triumphant slam or a sad set, and inside all that, as they talked, they were taking charge of my life as they knew it.

I had wondered a little why the only time I saw them, after the warmth and affection of summer, was on Sunday, when Charley brought me to their houses, to wherever the football game was being watched, cursed, bet on. Charley remembered to take me to the Canona Country Club to dances because he knew I liked to dress up. He said that it endeared me to him, and I took that as a declaration of love, hearing more than the words he said. Even that stopped. In early October, when we went up to the customary table they saved for each other, there was no place for us. We sat alone for a while and left soon, for the last time.

I had no idea that all of this was organized by Sadie until I met Kitty Puss in the parking lot where it had all begun. She was just pulling her MG out. She had chosen it because it was as near a good-old-days roadster as she could find. She said so. She stopped when she saw me and called me over and patted the blue side of the car and said, "Have you ever made love in a rumble seat or a duck blind or a horse stall? I have. God, it's uncomfortable, but then, you dance when the boys ask you or they won't ask you back. When in the hell are you going to wake up?"

I didn't dare ask what she meant, and she didn't wait. "They're up there on the hill in Sadie's living room right now getting sozzled over bridge and planning how to kill you. Why do you think nobody but me asks you for drinks anymore?" "Nobody" was her own small "age group," still bound by the rules of the sacred circle when they were growing up.

"They do," I said, thinking of my own friends. "I go when I can, but I'm working, too . . ."

"Not my friends, kid, and not Charley's. They've done this before, run women out of town who got too close to Charley Bland. He won't stand the pressure. He never has. He ain't worth a hill of beans." She looked straight ahead. "Oh, God, beloved Charley Bland; he gets in your mind and he won't let go. You leave town. That's my advice you didn't ask for, but you've got more to do than hang around here. What it is I've never bothered to find out."

She slid the MG past me and I stepped back. "He won't marry you, you know, he never does," she called back, for the whole parking lot to hear, and then gunned her way into the street, daring anyone coming to hit her.

Kitty Puss was right. She usually was.

In November the squirrel season started, more important to my neighbors, who were hungry but would have admitted it to nobody, than to the silk-stocking Democrats who surged to the polls, proud of electing a President they saw as being like themselves, caring but *chic*. The men from the hollows were in the woods, sitting still under the high trees before dawn, waiting for the flick of movement, the telltale streak of gray fur down the trunks, the color in winter of the gray squirrels.

I could hear the crack of their guns, fired so seldom, not wasting a shot. When I had said I noticed this, my neighbor Derwent said, "We don't shoot like them fellers you know. Them bullets cost ten cents apiece."

By early December, on the high pass in the winter wind, the pipes froze, and the snow piled against the walls, and Jubal and I were alone for day after day in the great expanse of white stillness outside where the road was hidden and there were no tracks except those of the small animals that shared the high pass. My neighbors had gone to ground. The nights crackled with cold; the ice falling from the trees was like someone shooting in the dark outside.

But the woods were ours again, and when the snow melted, and before it came again, I saw that the earth was never dead in what city people called the dead of winter; the advent of new life was there already, struggling up out of the soggy mast, a promise, and, as I still thought, a hope. There was even, on the few warm days, the smell of growing green shoots. Crows pecked at the dropped corn kernels, and got so used to Jubal and me that they didn't fly away. The squirrels took us as one of their own. Nothing else moved as far as we could see along the high pass.

We walked the forgotten fairways of the golf course, gone back in the gray days of winter to its centuries of silence. In these blessed necessary days and nights, I was finding the taproots of my search for the past, and nobody in that cruel time knew what discoveries they had led me to.

Charley came to the cabin less and less, and I was forced too many times to skid down the mountain road alone for food or for one of the days of tutoring in French I had started as a way to earn a living.

As Christmas came nearer, I drove through the noisy streets of red-and-green festoons of paper, of bells and lights, into the blessed darkness of the mountain road, to walk with Jubal in the lowering night. We knew the fields and the golf course so well that we walked into moonrise unafraid. Jubal checked back, and hightailed along the fairways, a dog of habit for his pleasures.

We walked from the fourteenth green, nearest us at the edge of the course, along the rough, where the birds had come back between the trees, to the clubhouse, where there were lights for the few members avid enough to be playing golf before dusk. I felt like a wild animal myself, out in the dark, unseen, unknown, free in the early night.

By mid-December a tall Christmas tree had been put up in the ballroom, and the colored lights splashed the snow outside. The great glass wall looked like a television screen. Jubal and I, across the empty swimming pool and up a slight hill, paused under an oak tree. The Christmas tree was tame in the distance; the wild oak had been freed by careful landscaping of its centuries of close neighbors. It had spread its arms like a blessing over the ground, making a shelter and a hiding place.

One night when we went there, or when Jubal went and I followed, unconcerned and happy, along the snow-studded winter grass, watching the stars, I ran into a wall of noise. It was the sound of a thousand birds, and I thought, We have an invasion of crows, that high scree of voices.

But then I saw the headlights, the twin lights against the blackness, the way they had been so long ago when Bobby Low told me about the animals' eyes, as the cars came in a line up the mountain road. It was a Christmas party.

Nobody should be left out of anything at Christmas. It is a sin against the time. But Christmas parties among the genteel are a way of stating who you are and whom you know, of paying back a year of drinks, of invitations, the kinds of parties where you go in the door and check, without being conscious of it, who has been dropped, left out, damned and sunk during the year.

I watched them for a long time and my eyes sheeted over with tears. I wiped them away, afraid to move from the oak tree, Jubal beside me. They were strangers, I was sure they were strangers, it was just that it was Christmas and I was getting lonelier and the stern attitude that I had developed that being alone was a blessing and not a curse was not quite working.

The snow on the terrace was flecked with patches of color from the lights, but the evening had grown warm and by the next day, I knew, there would be no snow, and I comforted myself that Charley Bland would come up on the mountain and stay with me a while. He didn't like to drive when the snow was on the road, for fear of being caught there by winter and, I suppose, by me.

Jubal bounded away before I could catch him, danced around the cup of darkness where the empty swimming pool lay, and up the other side onto the terrace. I was trying to call him without making noise. It was cold standing still, and I wanted to move away, away from reminders of what was happening, and back into my darkness and the fast walk toward home across the high ridge where the lights were stars. I didn't want to be caught there, grizzling and watching. I was ashamed of myself.

Then I saw why he had run. It was Charley Bland. He had stepped out onto the terrace from the party, and I saw him light a cigarette, the tiny burst of his lighter, the glow in the distance a point of still fire. He was wearing his new gray-on-gray houndstooth jacket; he bought one every year when the man from Chipp came to town. The white shirt that was the only kind he ever wore gleamed in the lights from inside.

I could even see what tie he wore. It was his favorite; he called it his Sunday-go-to-meeting tie, thin that year, blue with a dark stripe, the same one he had spilled a drink on and that his mother had had cleaned for him. She said the blue matched his eyes. Charley Bland was dressed up fit to kill.

It was not a party of strangers. Kitty Puss had warned me and I hadn't listened. It was the aging sacred circle, moving around and around beyond the glass wall as they had done for years, until, like a lifespan of musical chairs, one and then another and then another would drop out to death.

Jubal bounded up to Charley and I heard him in the distance say, "Jubal, old boy." He leaned down and scratched him behind the ear.

I thought, He's going to know where he is, where we both are. He has come out to look, at least glance, toward the road where the cabin is. I waited to read something in his stance, his movement, to show me that he would rather be there than doing what I had seen as his duty, trapped by the others. I wanted to be reassured that his choice would have been the silence, the kindness, the love across the high pass.

But he did nothing at all. Nothing. Nothing in what he did told me that I existed for him just at that moment, even so near to where we had been happy. There was not even impatience, a twitch of a shoulder like the squirrels twitched, aware of hunters. He had come out only for a minute to smoke alone; his cigarette made an arc of light as he tossed it over the hillside. I was cold, colder than I ever remember being. I dared not move until he went back inside the glass wall.

Jubal waited for a minute on the terrace, confused, checking back, then watching the man inside. After too long he trotted back to me. I stood there, playing possum, while the party went on, watching from my oak tree, sanctioned or damned into freedom from them at last by their blind denial.

I knew then that Charley Bland was not trapped in either life he had chosen. He simply moved from one to the other, and while he was in one, the other did not exist. We did not, as I had thought, live parallel lives when we were not together. We were instead, in our own isolated tangents, totally separate, and he did not question that.

Years later I would put my fictional Jake Catlett under that tree watching, in the same year, 1960, as the children played inside, not knowing who he was or that he was, and I would give him unknowingly the fury and the hurt I felt when I walked the dead miles across the ruined golf course to my cabin.

Money

Money. It is most thought about, most effective, and least written about in stories about love. Who buys the groceries for lovers to eat? Who pays the rent, the gas for the car to get to the trysts?

You have to get there, you have to make it possible to stay, and you have, sometimes, even in this profane ecstasy, to eat, drink, and sleep. Money makes the mare go, as Jane Austen universally acknowledged. George Eliot knew the importance of Dorothea Brooke's seven hundred a year, which affected the whole theme of *Middlemarch*. As Bernard Shaw said, having his usual last word, it isn't money but lack of money that is the root of all evil.

Money. In the whole time that I shared the secret life of Charley Bland, it was never mentioned, either by him or by my family. I survived as I could in a turnabout from the years in Paris: translations of pop culture stories from French to English, fashion articles, and, once, a speech for the head of the Jaycees, for which I got fifty dollars.

It was all seen as genteel exercises. The tutoring I did for the children on the hill who were failing French was the sort of thing that ladies did. The long drives in Charley's borrowed hunting car, with its comforting smell of old dog, to give readings from my single novel, were understood as something vaguely between the spiritual weekends in North Carolina and sorties among the famous, though who the famous were supposed to be nobody ever asked.

Finding a cabin that cost eighty dollars a month, about a third of the cost of Charley Bland's Chipp jacket, had been seen as an artistic caprice. In all these ways the real need for money was ignored.

The savings I had and the money I could earn ran out, renewed, ran out again. More and more often I went down the dangerous road to the perpetual parties because there was no food in the house. I was losing weight. Women said I looked *fab*ulous, and wished they could do it; I was growing as thin and furious and silent as my hillbilly neighbors.

I was hungrier there, surrounded by relatives, friends, and money, than I had ever been in the years in Paris after the war, when we cared for each other, or ever would be again. I once mentioned money to my mother and she said, in the cute voice she used when she was embarrassed, "It looks like you're going to have to get a job in the ten-cent store, doesn't it?" She turned away, shocked that I had spoken about such a taboo subject, and began to tell me about a friend of hers who did or did not do something.

I wasn't listening. I was aware that my face was red and hot. I was deep into that same embarrassment which is genetic with us. Southern genteels refuse to admit they are poor—broke yes, poor no, is the romantic phrase—and I recognized it in my mother and myself. I had by then been made too tender by overwork and hunger, or I would have known better than to open a subject so obscene.

Charley Bland had, of course, not mentioned money since the first night, when he asked me if my father gave me any. It seemed that daily bread had nothing to do with romance, secret or otherwise.

By the spring I knew that it was time to leave the cabin and go down into the town, where I had some hope of making a living that would allow me to keep on with my pale attempts to write, more needed as a refuge and more frustrating than work had been before. I was too much alone after a winter on the mountain. I needed company. Debility and boredom, which I didn't want to admit, and had elevated for myself into a kind of residual sorrow, were causing small illnesses and too much self-concern.

I walked along River Street, where the family houses had been turned into funeral homes and insurance offices, searching for a place to live. I wandered along the street of my childhood, looking at upstairs windows to see what was empty, finding nothing.

I went back to the second street from the river. The convention still held that the nearer the river you were, the more your house cost. What I found there was more than I could hope to pay. I was moving farther and farther from the river, to where the alien houses were with their shuttered eyes, where nobody lived that I had ever known. I walked a history of the streets of the town that dwindled, as they moved nearer and nearer the mountain where the cemetery was, from rich to poor, from grand to thin and board and batten, where men sat on the narrow porches in their shirt sleeves drinking beer, with their feet propped up on the thin wooden railings, and watched me without interest as I passed. Inside, when the weather was warm, I could hear the soap operas and the voices of women.

One afternoon I met two friends of Charley we had sat with on the riverbank on lost nights when we were looking for Broker Carver, who was a kind of broken guardian angel to the vestiges of the wild and sacred boys left over from the twenties. We would find all three of them down below the bridge when they had run out of money and been thrown out of the Wayfaring Stranger. Charlie Estep, the owner and bartender, kicked them out when his rock-hard patience had been broken at last. It took a lot. When Charley was drunk, he said they had more wisdom than anybody else he knew.

Dub Wilson had gone to junior high school with me, and his best friend, Sam Cutright, was a distant cousin from what my mother called, with some derision, a withered branch of the family. He had once gone "away" to school, long years before, to a military school, I think, to pull him together. It hadn't succeeded. They were drunken exiles from their own relatives on the hill.

Dub and Sam and Broker Carver had last names like the neglected old streets we wandered on together, reminders that their own families had settled the valley and built the town, cornered the land market, opened the mines. Dub and Sam had been inseparable for so long that they had grown as alike as brothers. I would see them standing together on street corners, smiling faintly, watching the people go by, both of them looking like Stan Laurel.

We walked together along the back streets near the old railroad station, long since closed, where the houses were older, built after the Civil War, when the railroad came through. They had been grand in their time, when it was a fashion in the 1880s to live near the station, especially for the mine owners, who took the labor train to the mines upriver.

They were beautiful, not yet rediscovered as "old," hidden by vines and broken porches. Between some of them were vacant lots where there had once been houses that had burned down, or side gardens long forgotten in the weeds. We passed house after house on one of those streets that like an old log left halfway in creek water had begun to rot at one end. The end where the fine houses were was called Carver Street, but nearer the station, beyond the fine houses, but seeming still to cling to them for a security long lost, was where the name had been changed to Beauregard Street. The houses on Beauregard Street still had the clear glass lozenges.

Dub saw it first, a closed window with a rag of a curtain caught in it, waving like a little wilted flag. It was one of the narrow houses that had a neglected garden on one side and a new yellow brick wall on the other, where someone, a long time ago, had shored up the neighboring house.

The garden belonged to a woman who was sitting in a bathrobe in a deck chair among the weeds. She had a hole in her stomach and a tube running out of it. She was so fascinated by this miracle that she insisted on showing it to all of us, and we stood around her, trying to think of polite and nice things to say about the hole and the tube. She told us she was going to die pretty soon; there wasn't nothing more that could be done, the doctors had told her, and she said it as casually as she said that the second floor next door was empty, that the house was owned by some fella, she forgot who but she'd think of it before we left, and she produced a key from her ample bathrobe pocket and called cheerfully after us, "It's real nice."

I called back over the weeds, remembering, "Can I bring my dog?" and she yelled, "Hell, honey, what kind of people wouldn't let somebody bring their dog?" She was still muttering to herself as we opened the front door with its clear glass lozenge.

We climbed the stairs, with the spindled newel post and the slim railing, into an upstairs hall. The apartment had been made simply by closing and locking a few doors, so that when we went on we were in the kitchen. They had saved plumbing money by putting the kitchen next to the old bathroom. Beyond a narrow corridor that was new, painted instead of being wallpapered like the rest, there was what had been the front bedroom. I saw its wallpaper and had an instant vision of Genevieve sitting there at a dressing table that didn't exist, brushing her bright hair. I realized then that the memory I had kept of her room in the house in Kentucky had been too large. I had been so small, the dressing table so high, the windows so far from me.

Tender vines grew up the wallpaper, and pink roses, an atmosphere again of Coty's powder, eyelet embroidery, and lace. The curtain caught in the window had been white and frilled sometime, the kind of curtain poor genteel relations washed and ironed every month so they wouldn't seem poor mouth. It was a gray rag.

In the back, the wall between two small back bedrooms had been knocked down and the room was large, with windows looking out over the streets we had been patrolling at the back. On one side we could see the neighbor, carefully inspecting herself, and on the other, the yellow brick wall.

When I called one of my parents' friends, who owned the place, he said, "My God, honey, you don't want to live there! That's just rental property," and then, "Oh, I reckon you're looking for material for your stories." He had found, quickly, an understandable excuse that didn't have to do with money.

My neighbors helped me pile the early-American furniture, the borrowed bed, all my papers, on a U-Haul truck and rode down with me, glad of a ride into town, far less scared than I was at maneuvering the truck down the steep mountain road silky with spring rain. I drove it through the downtown streets, and when I waved at Plain George, who was waiting to cross Mosby Street, he looked at me, surprised, and didn't wave back. Later he said, "The damnedest thing happened to me the other day. I saw a truck driver looked just like you."

I did not realize until later that by moving to Beauregard Street I was as exiled from the hill as Dub and Sam. I had joined the outcasts.

The Devil's Garden

Every morning in the fall of the year, I took Jubal across the abandoned railroad tracks and up the hill to the cemetery to work him on the graveyard coveys. There were two of them. We walked among the graves through the early mist, and the yew trees in their blue-green dawn mist could have been painted by Monet. The town below us looked like a small French city then, with its confluence of two rivers, its church spires, and its houses that had moved with time up both hillsides away from the rivers. I could see their roofs, red and brown and gray pastel in the mist until the sun burned it off, and we went from France to Beauregard Street into the exile I was calling home.

When Charley's setter bitch, Birdy, came into heat, I offered Jubal as a mate. As beautiful, as well trained as he was, the Bland women wouldn't allow it. The symbolism I had missed was too much for them. She came on heat at the weekend. As soon as Charley went to work on Monday morning, Sadie let Mosby out, and with a joyful leap he jumped the kennel fence. He was too late. Dearie had already let her own son get to her. So Birdy, impregnated by both the family dogs, was due for a large and polyglot litter. Dearie said she would be the one to drown the pups; she always was.

So when Charley wanted to take me with him hunting, there was no question of slipping heavily pregnant Birdy out of her kennel. We took Jubal.

Without even discussing it, we knew we had to leave so early in the morning that no one would know we had gone. There were no cars, no people yet. There was the dawn cry of the birds, and when we left, Beauregard Street was still with night and the streetlights had just begun to turn pale. We drove up the river east toward the mountains into the morning. Cold fog seeped into the open windows, and the music on the car radio was true hillbilly, where people went away from their lovers forever on the train or the bus, and everybody was flat broke and drove a truck or worked at the sawmill.

Jubal leaned against the window to catch the morning wind. It combed the feathers of his ears. All the way up the river he sat, alert to the coming morning.

The car lights cut through the ghosts of fog on the mountain, not enough to hide the hairpin curves, but enough to make us seem to float up toward its crest through a tunnel of trees.

Charley stopped the car at Lover's Leap to let Jubal out. Jubal ran into the woods. Charley locked the car. He explained that as far into the mountains as we were—we hadn't passed a car for nearly an hour—the mountain boys had their own code. They didn't consider whiskey and guns left lying around stealing, more borrying. He reached for a sterling-silver flask that had been given to him in the thirties when he was an usher at a wedding and put it in the pocket of his hunting coat.

We were dressed as alike as twins in canvas coats and canvas trousers, heavy lined boots, quilted vests, red hunting caps, all old, of course, there are no new hunting clothes, all as plain as a pickup truck, all from Abercrombie & Fitch. Mine had lain waiting for me for years in my parents' attic.

We stood in the wind near the edge of the platform rock that jutted out over an ocean of space, high above the river gorge. It was called Lover's Leap, like so many cliffs over the gorges of the Alleghenies, for the myth of an Indian princess, always a princess, who had leapt with her lover. Like the hillbilly songs, mountain love always ends badly.

Ten yards below it, a smaller jutting cliff was called Temptation Rock in an early effort to control the wild woods by some brave Bible people. One of their descendants had crawled down the steep mountainside and written in large white letters on the rock JESUS SEES YOU.

Not loves you, not has mercy on you, but has in the mountains the all-seeing terrible eye, blind eye on a rock. There was a small weatherbeaten cross with a name on it at the side of the rock cliff where someone, a long time ago, had fallen.

The sun lifted over the eastern ridge as we stood there in the cold, and the upriver wind seemed to bring its light to the water below that was a wild river but, from where we stood, a shining thread around the base of the far mountain.

We drank from the flask and the bourbon warmed us

and we loved the place and the land, not as it might be, or it once was, but then, together on that morning on his favorite day of the year, when the hunting season opened and he said he began to live again. The frost had turned the whole mountainside into a bright harvest of red and yellow maples, and the darker red royal color of the oaks. Our faces were caught by the sun and we looked at each other, seeing ourselves mirrored in each other's face. We glowed with love and bourbon and the harsh upriver wind and the new sun.

Jubal came and stood beside us. The wind caught the feathers on his tail and his chest, and he raised his head to the sun, perfect in the morning. I said he reminded me of Bierce's man against the sky, which was based on the western campaign in the Civil War in the same mountains, and he said what was that? When I told him, he said, No, honey, that couldn't have happened, just a story. He rejected things that interfered with some dream inside him, which he had kept whole for so long.

At nine o'clock, we had been driving for two hours into the mountains. He parked his car at the mouth of the Devil's Garden. We walked into the hollow. It was a deep crevice that ran four or five miles back between the ridges, and then branched into two hollows that went on beyond where we had ever explored. Mountain hollows are deceptive. They fan out like the fingers of a splayed hand. If you hunt to the head of a hollow and then the ridge, you can turn into the wrong cutback down the mountain and end up miles from where you parked your car, tired and cold from walking all day.

The Devil's Garden was the most secret place we knew, a gift from an old man who had hunted it for thirty years.

Charley Bland

The hunters of the wildest of game birds, the mountain grouse, have their hidden places where the birds haunt the undergrowth and can get up almost in front of your feet with a terrifying whirr of wings that sounds like a jet plane taking off, or can lurk forever just beyond your range, appearing and disappearing in split seconds between the tree branches. They are the color of the woods and the fall, and they are so elusive that you cannot say that they are as elusive as another animal but that all animals must compare with them, as elusive as a grouse.

Wild grouse, unlike the silly pheasants that anybody can shoot, have such avian intelligence that when they have been hunted too much they become the most wily of fliers. They hear your quiet footsteps and can fool even a good grouse dog that hunts close, as Jubal had been trained to do. The men who hunt them have this quality, too; they guard their secrets and their secret territories.

He bestowed it on us as if he had given us a wedding present, a secret wedding present for a secret wedding for the most secret of hunters and of birds. He said being with us, hunting, kept him happy just to see us, and once, when Charley couldn't hear, he said, "For God's sake, don't leave him."

We walked slowly; I took the side of the hill. Charley took the old logging road that had made an Eden for hunters in the Devil's Garden, the bits of gravel long left beside the almost hidden path, the underbrush that had grown up years ago when the virgin trees were cut and hauled out of the hollow.

That morning the leaves and the air were a mist of gold. We moved through it, alight with it and with being there. We said nothing. I cradled the 20-20 from Belgium he had lent me. It was so light in my hand that I hardly felt its weight. He had bought it because he needed a small gun, but he disliked it as he disliked women. He said it was a ladies' gun.

He carried a 16-gauge. As we went deeper and deeper into the woods, he walked with the ease of a man who was going home. He lifted his face toward the sun like a blind man seeking warmth. He was so still, so happy, that he was hardly aware I was with him.

Slowly, making as little noise on the dry leaves as we could, we walked up the hollow in a mist of gold leaves and filtered sun. Jubal went on point a few yards ahead, and Charley signaled that it was my bird. I simply stood there and watched the grouse, on the low branch of a small tree that seemed too thin to hold its weight as it sat, its head to the cool sun as his had been, free, alone. The wind lifted its bronze and brown shining feathers. I stared until the bird flew away with a loud whirr of its brute wings. It was the longest pause for a mountain grouse that I would ever see, a full minute of stillness. I hadn't even lifted the gun.

He was too disgusted with me to speak. It didn't last. "All right, I know," he said. No more.

We got to the tiny valley where a thorn-apple tree grew in the middle of cinquefoil and lespedeza a mile inside the hollow. We sat on a log that the loggers long ago had left there. Toadstools grew at the end of it, and it smelled of damp and wood mast. We had sat there before, in better times, and it was still the same, still the quietness, still the peace, still even hope again, as if the world outside were benign.

He stared out at the hillside ten yards away, and I thought he was going to speak, but he didn't. He knew he didn't have to. I had seen him like that, quiet in the cabin, in my apartment, in motel rooms, once on the steps of one of those late-night lairs he went to for peace, where we stayed together so late at night that even the Moose or the Bear or whatever place it was had closed, and we sat down on the steps with no place to go.

He looked then as quiet as another man would in a favorite chair in his own home. He had never, he told me, found a place where he was comfortable at home unless his father was gone and he could take his chair. He told me that innocently.

This was no different from the other snatches of quietness he had found, but more. It was a worship of stillness.

Was it that time or another time, there were so many, a life lived together in the woods, that Jubal came and put his paw on Charley's knee to remind him where he was? Then he ran to the edge of the clearing and stood, then ran back, then repeated a dog dance of impatience, nose lifted to the scent of the woods and the birds.

Charley's head went up, too, and he allowed himself pure joy. It came out from him as laughter, a birdsong in the deep woods, as if he realized that at last he was safe from anything but joy. He looked beautiful, as people do at prayer. He glanced at me as if I were a stranger who had wandered there, and then his eyes refocused and he smiled at me, got up, and started after the dog.

The birds were wild that day, celebrating the first hard frost, the cold sun, the haunting breeze that reached down from the mountaintop and ruffled the gold leaves. That is the other secret of grouse hunters. It is the woods themselves, the place, the day, as much as the birds. It is a good day if there are one or two grouse near enough for a shot.

You may remember with other game birds what you have shot, but with the grouse you remember every bird you have ever missed. They linger there in your mind in that split second when they show themselves.

We stopped counting at seventy birds, and then we just walked, saying nothing. Jubal went on point over and over, just out of range, and we didn't care.

There was no time. We walked quietly, as wary as animals, stopped as they would stop at the faint crack of a twig. We found another log when the weak sun was overhead between the patches of gold underbrush. We ate a little, and he explained that it was too cold to eat much, that the blood went to your stomach, and your feet and hands froze.

There is a kind of bodily fatigue that is light, easy, like a blessing. We had walked to the head of the main hollow, about five miles, and turned for the first time into one of the forks, so deep in the mountains we might have been the first people there, and I thought, I know how Juno renewed her virginity. She went into the woods. That, too, was an illusion; there was third growth all around us and what was left of the logging road, almost obscured by mast and small bushes gilded by fall and the sun. We had to push the branches aside. It was as if we were walking through their light.

Jubal went on point, close up ahead. We both froze, like the dog. Charlie walked forward. The grouse roared up and hovered for a second that lasts forever between the bushes on both sides of the road. He shot. It tumbled out of the air. I can still see it, not tumbling, but paused there in the air.

Jubal brought it back, its wings moving in his mouth.

He dropped it into Charley's hands. He put it into his own mouth and turned his back on me. He didn't want me to see him bite its neck to kill it, but when he turned around he had a drop of blood on his lip. He brushed it away and put the bird in his poacher's pocket.

"It's better that way. Quick," he told me, and nothing more. We walked into the cool of the afternoon, into exhaustion that was no longer a blessing, and in the car, he handed me the flask and said, "Drink and get warm."

As I lifted it to my mouth he suddenly looked at his watch and said there was enough time. He had to pick up his mother's latest favorite visitor and take her to a dinner party. I handed the flask back and said I didn't want it, I wasn't cold. He had been watching the time, as I had not, as we walked back through the last glow of the day.

We didn't talk or play the car radio on the way back. We sat there in our separate places, driving toward the city, to punishments and expectations, to the other story, the public story.

I watched his face losing its glow as the day lost its glow into evening, grow smaller again, and grayer. The deep lines of control beside his mouth were back, and the preoccupied way he answered me when I tried to talk and recapture the day, until I, too, was quiet and tired and hopeless, driving back through the evening, back to the attrition of small habits and defeats, day after day after day.

November's Dark

I think that the experience of time is not in passage, in day after day, but in the awareness that it has gone, or the illusion that it is infinite. It was that way then. I knew that seasons changed and habits remained the same and people disappeared and their places in the scheme of things were taken by someone else, until their functions were filled and memory of them was censored and colored with nostalgia.

Six years passed, and what I did and what was done are distilled into scenes. Over and over I tried to get away, as I had done when I was adolescent. I remember driving my car across the border into North Carolina once, and suddenly stopping by the side of the road, suffused with relief that my mind had escaped the private love of Charley Bland almost all the way across the mountains, and what an emptiness it was, a joy.

I tried to get away from what public love had become

by clinging to the book I was trying to write. I retired into that place untouched and saved by work. The place they had allowed for me hardly existed anymore. I was a shadow in both their houses.

But Charley Bland always reeled me back to give him more time, give him more peace, be there, just be there in that trap of veils he called his life. He would call me, late at night, wherever I was, and talk to me for an hour at a time, hotel-room talk, private promises that he would do something, loving and free and secret. In a hotel room in some college town where I was speaking, in a retreat where I was trying to work, I would watch shadow after shadow on the walls of all those places, strange pictures, strange wardrobes, strange mirrors reflecting alien rooms that had become a safety for me, with night after night outside the windows, winter and summer, snowfall, moon, and rain, all reflected in the memory of his voice, the words that were a blessing to me, a habit to him, "Please. I long for you." I went back, every time, and nothing had changed.

There was, I know now, another reason, as deep as a taproot. For better or for worse, this was my country, and I could not let it go until it blessed me. What form that blessing would take I did not know yet. I only knew that when it came I would recognize it through its disguises. It is this that keeps poets in their countries through name-lessness, doors closing, hungers, and there are many kinds, until they are forced to abandon home, which can, in itself, become a *felix culpa*, a blessing.

There is a place—time is a place, too—where you are allowed to go, really go, and your leaving is its own clean blessing. It makes the escape to breathe and then return, knowing that in your heart you have not left at all, into a parody. That place of release had not yet come. I knew this, and I waited.

Things had changed on the hill. My father had died when I was away on one of my escape attempts. Nobody but Charley Bland knew where I was, and he did not think to tell my mother. His habit of secrecy was too strong. So my father, who had been on the edge of my life for so long, had already been buried when I came back.

In my mother's terrible isolated mourning for him, I was caught in her habits and her despair. I went back to live for a while on the hill with her. We played Scrabble until late at night when the light in Charley Bland's bedroom had long gone out. Then the next stage of her mourning came, and her friends were called onto the hill in the evening to play canasta, so the evenings were filled and she took a sleeping tablet when they had gone.

But when I thought that the place of my father was being patched together in her, I would glimpse her, trying to face the town, almost staggering along the street like an old old woman, so heartbreakingly dressed in pride and new clothes that she looked as if she were going to a wedding.

She never talked about him at first, and then he, thirty years old again, began to come into her thinking that came from her mouth as words, unfocused on anyone but with me there to hear, as if he were alive, and safe at last, sometimes as she would have liked him to be, and sometimes, disguised as "funny" stories, resentments of him I had never known she had.

It was said in her family then that they were so deeply in love that they should never have had children, since they lived only for each other. It was true. In her new life with the dead there was no room for me, only her own and only love reiterated in the night, so that I would run in and hold her while she sobbed; she didn't register who it was.

Gradually feeling was coming back, as into a frozen hand, and it hurt the same way, and she struck out at me, who was in the way of the life with my father lodged there in her mind at thirty, before I was born. I remained useful to do things, play Scrabble, change light bulbs, but I myself no longer pleased her.

Her plans had not worked out. She was contemptuous and sad for me because I had not married Charley Bland as she had intended. She said that it would have been the least I could do for her when she needed me. One evening, when he came for me there, his family safely away, I found them in the living room, and she was flirting with him. "*I* would have brought him to heel," she said later, believing it.

The time came when she no longer talked incessantly about my father. I would have expected her then to go back to the old refrain about "your grandfather." But she did neither.

It was her self, which she had put aside a long time before, that she picked up again, free of her father, my father safe at thirty in her dreams, I an eighteen-year-old again that she "couldn't do a thing with." I could hear her telling her two oldest friends this when they played canasta, their shrill voices surging down the stairs while I sat in the early-American kitchen in the basement, trying to work.

As if she had been interrupted in her reading, she picked up where she had left off. She began to read again, not the Waverley Novels, one of which she had always kept by her bedside to honor her father. She withdrew into first editions of Edith Wharton that had been forgotten on the bookshelves years before. She read Elinor Wylie and Edna St. Vincent Millay, and talked to me about them as if I were a stranger.

She hinted that it was time I moved back down into my apartment. She was sure I would be happier there. She had enough company in her dog and her friends, she said, and she knew I had other things to do. We had always had a dog, and it was always hers. It was too old, she told me, to share with Jubal. "Territory, you understand," she said, talking about the dog.

She said she couldn't possibly do without Bounce, she was used to dogs at home. She never used the word "home" for any place where we were actually living, only for the large house in the middle of what had once been a farm and had become a coal town, where she was born. The dog there was always called Bounce.

One day Bounce, who was old, didn't get out of the way of the mail truck in time. She cried harder for Bounce than she had for my father, as if the child in her had given her permission to cry for a pet when the conventions had measured the tears for the human dead. She couldn't stand tears in other people or in herself. She said she'd seen enough of that, when and where she never told. But when she called me to tell me what had happened, she touched the heart of her truth. "Now I don't come first with anybody," she sobbed.

In the Bland living room, where the griffins fought in the medallion cages of the old carpet, there had been a change, too. The room had grown a little scruffy with age. There was an untidiness that Mrs. Bland refused to notice, a glass ring on a polished table left there from one week when I went for dinner to the next when I went back. My summons to dinner had shrunk and were always, she explained, because he, not calling Mr. Bland by name anymore, wanted to talk to me. The magazines that had been so meticulously stacked were piled haphazardly; there was dust in the corner beyond Mr. Bland's throne.

Randolph had left sometime in those years, and there was a series of slovenly boys who banged down the silver tray and threw logs on the fire so hard that sometimes sparks exploded and landed on the griffin carpet.

There was death in that house, too, but each death leaves a different space behind it. It was not one of the aged triumvirate. The two sisters had grown a little younger, as people do when they go into their eighties, and Mr. Bland more honest and less regarded in the evening ceremony. It had been poor Cuddy, who I would have thought would have been the least missed. He left more emptiness to maneuver and fill than I ever would have thought he could, and he would certainly have not imagined it, had he had imagination, in his life.

He had died of a cerebral hemorrhage in his car, driving down Mosby Street to All Saints Church. Sadie grabbed the wheel and swore at him when the car veered, so that the last words he heard from this world were "You damned fool, watch where you're going." She kicked his foot aside and slammed hers down on the brake just as they met a tree trunk. She went to the funeral looking like the brave drummer boy, which was somehow right for her, with a bandage on her forehead where she had hit the windshield. Cuddy's blood had flown out and soaked the steering wheel and Sadie's hands and her linen dress. It was in summer.

She told them all this in tears, over and over in the first

week of his death, so that Charley said Mr. Bland finally told her to pull herself together, that she was not the only one who had lost Cuddy, as if he had been misplaced. For a while, in conversation and in roles, they seemed to search for him in a desultory way.

When I walked up the barn road to Sadie's house to make my visit of condolence—fifteen minutes, no more, no less, was the rule on the hill—I saw her through the glass wall beyond the *Monstera deliciosa*, playing bridge with Daisy and Maria and Melinda. The inevitable glasses of bourbon were at the corners of the table. They were taking her through the dark voyage of her mourning the only way any of them knew how to do, at the same table where they had planned my defeat so long ago. I could see them there, day after day after day, dealing cards until she was ready to ride again. I walked on by.

Instead of the waters closing over Cuddy's memory, since he seemed to have made hardly a stir in his life, the family changed places and parceled out, almost consciously, Cuddy's usefulness. Mr. Bland fell to talking to me about the coal business, since, as he said, my family knew about such things better than his did. He glared over my head at the rest of the family, who sat around the fire paying no attention to him or to me anymore. He said they were like a bunch of hogs who lay around under an oak tree eating the acorns and never looking up to see where they came from.

The standoff between Mr. and Mrs. Bland reminded me of the Smallweeds in *Bleak House*, only they didn't throw cushions at each other. They played at ignoring each other, constantly trying like children, at the same time, to get a rise. Mr. Bland would read the *Times* and scatter it across the carpet and leave it there for her to notice, but she never did, not in front of him. "I wouldn't give him the satisfaction," she said once to me—I remember that because she so seldom directed a remark to me anymore.

So Mr. Bland and I would sit in the ceremonial corner with the papers strewn around us and he would talk about the coal business, as he was sure, he told me, he had always talked to Cuddy. He was sure he had done this, when I had hardly heard him exchange a word with Cuddy. "I miss him," he said, and his old eyes that looked like dirty glass watered a little, not much.

So I alive became Cuddy dead, an ideal Cuddy who had listened to him as I did, and he talked on, not waiting for me to answer, which was a blessing, since I had so little to say. I would find myself reading headlines on the sports page on the floor.

Mrs. Bland, who had paid so little attention to Cuddy in his life, did not mourn him at his death. I respected that in her, although it was her most dangerous virtue. She had never seen the need to lie about anything she did, and she saw no reason then to grow sentimental about someone she had hardly seen. She kept him alive in the conversation for a while, referring to "what Cuddy would have thought, what Cuddy would have liked" out of a politeness to the dead.

It was simpler for Charley Bland. There was an empty place that he was expected without words to fill. He became, for all of them, the only son Mrs. Bland had considered him to be for her all his life. He was moved, like a chessman, without any conversation, permission, or choice on his part, across the board of the living room into the place of husband-as-escort for Sadie, and she, a little smaller, a little quieter for a while, still was concentrated on the point she had been all the time, unchanged, on Mr. Bland's face turned away from her, looking to him for the acceptance that she had longed for so long, in and out of Cuddy's frailer life.

It was only Dearie who truly mourned Cuddy the man, and I realized it was because they had both been together on the outside staring in for so long that now she was alone in a way none of the others were. She had grown smaller than Mrs. Bland, and something of the picture in the attic, a smile, questing some approval and acceptance, was left on her face, a sign that her private world, where she stayed almost entirely, was a happier one in nostalgia than it had ever been when she lived it. She sat in the same place, in the shadowed corner of the sofa, dutifully, every evening. She looked like the picture, but left out in the weather too long. She had taken to cutting her sparse hair the same way again.

One night Charley and I came in from late January. We had been, for one of those blessed times between work and evening, at the Wildcat, where the jukebox played "Railroad, Steamboat, River and Canal" and the only wine was Blue Nun.

There is so much dark within us, still crouched around the campfire, letting no strangers in. The house was that way that night, closed against the winter. From the driveway, where the air was thin and cold and the frost crunched under our feet, with the bare trees, abandoned by their leaves, stark against the welcoming brightness from the windows, and the smell of smoke from the logs burning that came from the chimney, it was, that night, a haven.

We shook out of our coats in the silent hallway, and Charley went first into the living room. I followed. Mrs.

Bland presented a cold cheek. Mr. Bland said, "Will you have a drink or have you already had one?" Dearie stared at the window as if she were thinking of running for it, and Sadie didn't look up from her magazine.

I think they have stopped there ever since in my mind, just that way, at a perpetual seven o'clock, waiting for somebody to tell them to come into the dining room, Dearie smiling at nothing, Charley leaning on Mrs. Bland's chimneypiece, watching the fire through his drink, Sadie reading *Town and Country*, Mrs. Bland's hand lifted above a needlepoint she seemed never to finish.

I was staring at the fire and finding pictures I still see. Mr. Bland, in the middle of some story he was telling about No. 10 seam, kicked the tray so hard that the bourbon bottle flew halfway across the room, and the ice sprayed in the air, and two of the glasses crashed against the stone hearth.

He yelled, "Goddamnit, keep your head down," and collapsed back into his chair, his face the color of Silly Putty some child had played with too long with dirty hands. He was watching the ceiling intently when I turned back to him, one hand wiping the thrown bourbon from my skirt. His leg kept twitching, and his head was still moving. All of this, as death does, took only a few seconds.

Mrs. Bland yelled back, "Look what you've done!" The messiness had finally gotten to her, but it was too late. Mr. Bland was never going to hear another voice.

He lasted a week in a coma, and then he went out with the night, as Dearie told me, in hospital, all that was left of that small elegant feisty man hooked up to machines when he should, as a man of his time, have died in the tester bed, still giving orders to a family he didn't have much use for.

I lay on my sofa all afternoon the cold day he died,

knowing a brute truth so heavy it held me there, mourning his loss. The hours passed without hope. With his death, my last ally in that dry font of promise was gone, and I knew it with my whole heavy silent body. The snow fell all day long, softly outside the window, down the yellow brick wall, or was that another time? In every time of loss in that place I remember snow drifting down the blank wall. It was so still within that despair of recognition that I could hear my own heart beat, until at last it was night and the wind rose and flailed at the window and drove the snow across the wall.

One week after Mr. Bland was buried, Sadie made Charley buy her house, packed up her furniture, including a mounted fox brush and a fox head she had won at Aiken, hitched a horse box to the back of her BMW, and she and her horse lit out for Lexington, Kentucky, where she had been trying to persuade Cuddy to go for years.

She was married three months later to a rich man with the acres she had seen only in what she had made of Mr. Bland's stories about the good old days in Spotsylvania County. She, quite truly, lived happily ever after. I met her years later on Fifth Avenue and she greeted me as if we had been friends and told me all this standing in front of Saks. She looked taller, slimmer; the belligerent squareness had gone out of her face. She had joined at last, and with obvious zest, the people Turgenev called the rich, the happy and unjust, and she had paid her dues and didn't give a damn. Some door she had knocked on for so many years had finally opened for her. She didn't even mention the Bland family, which had held her in thrall with promissory notes of love for so long.

In that same week Charley Bland disappeared. I hadn't

known it. I had taken for granted he was on the hill being part of the days after death that were so formal there, but he wasn't. Finally Mrs. Bland had to call me.

"I can't find Charley." Her naked voice on the phone sounded like a lost child's. "I've tried every place," and with that terrible honesty of hers—"I didn't want to call you, but I don't know what else to do. Cuddy isn't here or Partlow, and Sadie had to leave me just when I needed her . . . I called Plain George, and he doesn't know." Of course, he wouldn't. He had protected Charley from her for too many years to give up that honor. Then, with a turn into a new thought, she said, "I wish you would come up again and talk to me like you used to. I don't have anybody . . ."

I lied, too, and said I didn't know where Charley was, but I did. I knew the place that was his abyss, and so did his dearest friends, and it had usually been Plain George, of course, who had gone and rescued him. This time I didn't wait to find Plain George. I went myself. I stuffed his shaving gear, his toothbrush, his change of underwear, and a clean shirt he kept at my apartment into the briefcase I usually used for manuscript. I didn't, even though it was far too late, want to be seen going into the Henry Hotel with a suitcase, as if it mattered.

I walked into the dirty Edwardian lobby with its lofty ceiling dim with naked 40-watt bulbs, where the gilt was still streaked on the high columns from the day when Ellen Terry had stayed there, and Lillie Langtry and all the others, and now, in the butt-sprung chairs, abandoned men sat behind the morning papers. There was a sense of everybody waiting for some evening that never was going to come, and if it did was not going to bring what they were waiting for.

The clerk had seen me there with Charley so many

times that he had the key in his hand when I went up to
the desk. He said, "I wish you'd get him out of here. There've
been complaints." Who in that place would have reason to
complain of anything he did, that they had done themselves
so often, I didn't ask. Perhaps there were innocent strangers,
driving through the town, who landed there without knowing that it was a home from home for half the men from
the genteel citadels along the opposite hill.

Charley Bland lay on the floor on the brown worn rug
of the corner room, the room we always went to. His breathing was beyond snoring, a dragging in and out of air. He
had dirtied himself. When I knelt down, he smelled like a
sewer. He wasn't asleep or passed out. He was crying, soft
little whimpers that had once been gusts of tears.

I helped him up. "Where the hell have you been?" he
muttered to the floor. "Why did you wait so long to come?"
Someone knocked on the door. It was a black waiter bringing ice. When Charley lurched backward to let him in, he
stumbled and fell again. The waiter kicked him aside, hard,
in the ribs, and said, "You son-of-a-bitch," before he saw
me. He didn't apologize.

He said instead, "You oughtn't to be here. This ain't no
place for a woman." When I made a move toward him,
maybe I was going to protect Charley from another kick as
he went out, maybe I was so furious I was going to hit him,
he said, "Don't bother. He done give me fifty dollars to look
after him," and he was gone, the door slammed behind him.

Charley had drunk himself into that appalling reality
he seemed to seek. I got him into the shower and held him
there. He kept saying, "He didn't leave me a damn thing."
In one of those switches into false sobriety he told me
calmly, leaning against the shower wall, letting the water

course over both of us, "Know who had most of the money? No, you don't. You don't know. You don't listen. Cuddy, old Cuddy, he was the one who had made most of the money. Papa Father Daddy was keeping Mother in the style she wished to be accustomed to on capital. There is only enough for her and to keep the house going. Oh boy, keep the house going. Keep the fifty-year-old ancestral mansion going for the descendants who don't exist at all costs. They made me buy Sadie's house on a mortgage to keep it in the family. I don't even like Sadie's house. There goes our chance, old fellow."

He tried to kiss me without any warmth, almost a slap, and he missed me and lurched against the door of the shower. It changed the direction of what he was saying. "Did you bring me some underwear? Throw that damned stuff out." He knew I had. I had done all of this before. Then he began to cry again. "Not a damn thing. I always thought there would be a time . . . I haven't saved a red cent. No reason to. I took for granted . . ." His voice trailed off and he went to sleep, a normal sleep, on the bed.

I called Mrs. Bland. It was too late for lying, too late to save her feelings, but the years of protecting her from the facts of life had been useless all the time. She knew where he was. "There wasn't anybody but you to go and get him. That corner room," she said. "I always see the light on when he hasn't come home, and say a little teeny-weeny prayer that he'll be all right."

She gave me my orders calmly in her grownup voice. "Let him sleep a while and then bring him home."

But she didn't forget that she had wanted me to come back at teatime. She called a day later and thanked me for

Charley Bland, as if I had delivered a parcel instead of a man broken by a bender. "Please," she said, "I've missed you." I never knew during those few weeks whether she would be child or lady or farm girl. I did know that like my mother she grew young with grief, and wise.

Those were the first weeks of the early spring, that time that seems never to end, a time of broken promises, when the sun brings out the first shoots in a day, and the wind beats them, and the afternoons turn gray.

"Nobody helped me at all," she complained, still a little girl that first day, with a gale blowing outside that made her shrug her shoulders from time to time as if the wind were jostling her. "Nobody. I read late at night." She leaned over to me, in the same chair where I had seen Mr. Bland begin to die, and touched my hand, leaving hers there, as cold as ice, her skin dry. "I am not sleeping a wink," she announced. "I leave the light on and all I have now are some fools who haven't told me what I want to know. I want to know why and they won't tell me." She became a child suddenly and the tears glistened in her eyes but didn't fall. "The Bible certainly doesn't do any good," as if all the world of literature and grace were gathered there to stanch a wound.

"Even Emily Dickinson won't tell me why and she has never let me down before. Although"—she waited for a pause, judging Emily Dickinson—"don't you think she was a little oversensitive? I don't trust sensitive people. They're just egoists anyway. Never think about anything except their own selves and their own feelings. What about us?"

What inner pictures of people she was seeing and judging I couldn't know, except that when she came back to me from her watchfulness of the wind out the window she said,

"You are far too sensitive for your own good. Impatient, too." What she had not said hung there between us. Charley and I had, in her words, been "courting" for six years.

For a few weeks she looked drab and small and weightless, a woman of eighty-five left over in her chair, and then, it seemed in a day, she began to rally, and talk about Mr. Bland. Like my mother had my father, she talked about a younger man. It was the next stage of her mourning and she was a young girl.

There had been nothing sentimental about her. "I taught school up in Botetourt County," she said, smoothing her dress in her lap and straightening up to look the way she must have then, starched shirt, small black tie, that fine white hair chestnut, she told me once, full and shining and pinned back to make her look older. "I wasn't much older than most of my pupils. Sixteen years old. Good grief." She had touched the fact and then she withdrew into being a lady again. "Papa told us that if we were going to take from the county we ought to pay back, so we all volunteered, even Dearie.

"So when Partlow came along, we used to say down the pike, when Partlow came down the pike"—she was almost gay about this—"oh my, I did loosen my hair so I would look prettier, and he would notice me instead of Dearie, who was the beauty of the family. And he did. He said" —she was shy again—"that I was brave. Of course, that wasn't exactly what I wanted to hear, but that was exactly what he was looking for. He didn't have a red cent then, but his uncle over here in West Virginia had done well"— with a little cough—"and he had come over to work for him. Well, he went up the hollows with a rifle under his arm and bought up coal leases; he was soon on his own, nothing would stop Partlow. By the time he brought me over, he was riding a big bay gelding that was beautiful and he had bought a house right in town, you know, Potter Street. I thought it was coming to heaven, even if it was West Virginia instead of east Virginia and my father said I was going among traitors, at least it was mine after that house with fifteen people coming and going and borrowing my things.

"The one thing I set my foot down about was having to live up at the mine. I'd lived on one cliff above the Jeams with only a footbridge that scared me to death when I went to school and I was not about to live on another. So Partlow was more than happy to ride the labor train. He kept his horse at the Laceys' stable. Oh, Lord, they were giants in the earth when I first came here. Those girls, the Bland girls, our cousins—" She gave another little cough to register the kinship, and then laughed a little at something she didn't say.

The afternoons seemed to bring back the color to her usually rosy cheeks, and the first daffodils were up. Charley was at ease again, at least in our private time. He would lounge in his favorite chair at my apartment and read, too, just letting himself heal and get ready, he said. What he was getting ready for he never said, and I couldn't know. With Sadie gone, he let himself be forgotten for a little while by the other women on the hill, and for us, it was the first peaceful time in years.

No, not peaceful, a blessedly empty time when we were left alone. My mother had gone to Europe, his mother and Dearie wandered around with some growing relief that nothing, for a while, was being expected of them. In March they took a Caribbean cruise.

Charley Bland

In military funerals in England, the slow march is played to the grave, a mournful dirge heard over the fields, then there is silence, and then, away in the distance, the quick march comes back toward your hearing, a rollicking tune, and a fine step, the death over, the mourning done.

On the fifteenth of April, when the rain soaked the daffodils, I went as usual to her house—it had become her house then in all our minds—to give her talk and tea, and as I stepped into the door it was like a new place. The hall was bright, the huge bowl of daffodils made their own light, the carpet was so clean it looked new, and when I stepped into the living room, the lady I had almost forgotten sat there, everything around her as tidy as when I first saw her there, ready to entertain. The devil's work ball, uncovered again, sat in its black lacquer stand, the needlepoint was folded where it had not been left for a long time, the *Connoisseur* and the *Antiques* were neat on the windowsill.

Mrs. Bland was herself again.

The room was lifted into the light by color, strong color. My dear carpet I had looked at for so long was gone. Across the floor the carpet was thick, dark red, blue, shot with yellow, its pattern as formal as a dance. It was not beautiful. It was rich.

"I hated that old thing," she said when she saw me pause. "I always wanted a decent carpet. Do you know, when I got the man from Richmond to appraise it, *it wasn't even real.*"

I could see the old carpet as an ephemeral shadow on the floor, as it is still, unreal except in my own mind. "We'd been lied to all those years. He didn't bring the thing back from abroad. He bought it in Fredericksburg." She sounded as if that was the last insult.

There was something else missing from the polished room, and I couldn't at first see what it was. We sat there in the mingled smells of newness—new carpet, new lemon-scented polish, a new tea she was trying out, new spring daffodils there, too, Dearie down over the hill with her dog for the first time that spring that she could get out of the house in the afternoon, a new space beyond the porch where the Queen Elizabeth rose had been. She followed my eyes. "I always hated that, too," she said. "Pour the tea. I have to talk to you."

At first I hardly paid attention to what she said. She was being wary, entering into a search for the right words. "Things," she said, "were bound to change. We have to be prepared for such things . . ."

I knew what it was. In that formality, where everything stayed the same, *The New York Times* was gone and there was still an unfilled space of habit where it usually lay on the windowsill, already read by her and folded for Mr. Bland. She saw me look there, too. She was missing nothing. "Oh, I got rid of that," she said, "it piles up so. And after all, what is there in the *Times* I need to know?"

"Now"—she seemed to find her voice—"you and Charley . . ." I was still and cold. Our names said together had been taboo for such a long time, even in conversation, and God knows, no recognition of any other coupling always had been.

"He's older now," she said, trying to be delicate when it was too late, "and he needs, well, things less than he used to. There's really so little you can do for him anymore. I think you have to consider how selfish it is to cling to something, anything . . ." Having touched so gently on the fact that in their formal world a man of fifty-one didn't "need" sex anymore, she was running out of words; all this was obviously hard for her, but she was, as Mr. Bland had said so long ago, a brave woman.

Then she saw my face and it annoyed her and gave her ammunition to go on. "Don't look like that. That's what I mean. You are too sensitive," and she said again, "It's nothing but a form of ego." Ego. The word hung in the air, and being old, she was suddenly tired of the conversation and of me.

"I am going to need Charley more now that there's nobody else. Surely you must understand that. What I am trying to get you to see is . . ." She never said, or I never heard her. I got up as carefully as I could, so that I wouldn't kick the silver tray, and said goodbye as politely as if I didn't know her.

"I'll call you when I need you for tea again," she called after me. I walked away down the hill, forgetting that I had left the car Charley had lent me. Charley's dog, Birdy, followed me all the way to the bridge across the river before I knew she was there and made her go home.

The mourning was over. The quick march had been played. Mrs. Bland, in one day, had gotten rid of what was blocking the way she wanted to go—the Queen Elizabeth rose, *The New York Times*, the old griffin carpet, and me.

Derby Party

Of course, the seeds of the end of all this were planted at the beginning, but I could not or would not see it then. I was like a child that knows night is coming and tries to hold it back by refusing to turn on a light, thinking the light itself makes the darkness. For once, my mother, whose timing was usually better than that, called, "Fool," both too late and too soon. She said she could have told me "all along." She had forgotten, or chosen not to remember, the parking lot.

But there it was, in the same house, the same room, the place where private and public love met in celebration, for a single day, at the beginning. It was where both of Charley Bland's lives met, too, and had for years.

For one day in the spring he dropped his habits of secrecy and his induced necessities. There, at first, everyone we knew seemed pleased for us. Later, in the same room, at the same time in spring, we went through the growing dissonance of one long afternoon, extended through the years we were together.

All over the South, from the eastern Piedmont to west of the mountains where the hills run into Kentucky, flowing in a circle, outward and outward, as if a stone were thrown in the water, there is an unofficial holiday. As it gets nearer, the visions return, as they have the year before and the year before that, familiar traditional names that foreshadow that few minutes at five o'clock, on the first Saturday in May, at Churchill Downs, when the Kentucky Derby is run.

The ghost of Gallant Fox with the ghost of the great Earle Sande up, War Admiral, the son of Man o' War, Whirlaway, the son of Equipoise, all of the three-year-olds that have ever won, whirl to their haunting finishes every year in the memories of the Kentucky Derby.

Old stories surface—the year the filly won, '29 when the track was wet, '35 when it was too dry, a grandfather who had an entry, someone who knew a famous jockey, my mother's reputation for picking winners. As the first Saturday in May drew nearer, the voices grew louder.

Every year the old days were mourned, when it had been a family of people who saw each other only once a year, when all the horses were Kentucky-bred, when there were no horses owned by syndicates, and every year for me, wherever I was, I could hear a long-dead Bobby Low say, "Bet the jockey." The Southern mountain soul rode that race; it was theirs.

On that Saturday, as he had for years, Charley Bland threw wide his arms, and controlled by no man or woman either, he celebrated the running of the Derby as if it were the first day of his life. All that joy he showed so seldom surfaced then, and innocently and honestly at first, it was the one place in the town that people wanted to be when "My Old Kentucky Home" drifted like a lost song across Churchill Downs.

He told me about his first Derby party. His parents were away and he was fourteen, and they huddled around a Crosley radio and drank bootleg whiskey and hoped that the voice of whoever announced from Churchill Downs would not fade at the finish. He won five dollars on Clyde Van Dusen, sired by Man o' War.

Later, there were small, then larger screens of the television, first in black and white and snow, that he rented for the day and put in the living room, the library, and, if the weather was right, out on the terrace. The first time I went, in 1960, Churchill Downs was bright green and red in that early, raucous color.

On that day he had taken as his own, Charley invited whom he wanted, even though each year he had to listen to and ignore the pale mewings of his mother, and the comments of Sadie, that usually began with "Why in the world . . ." and he always answered, "It's my party." Sadie said it was to pay back his "social engagements" of the year; Mrs. Bland said it was because he had acquaintances who had no television set, and wasn't it sweet of him to take all that trouble.

He insisted on inviting everyone himself, by telephone, afraid that someone would be left out if he didn't do it. His secret friends, polished for that one day, and a little shy, were greeted by Mrs. Bland as if she were at church.

I went for the first time only four weeks after I had come home, and only a week after I had become a part of Charley Bland's secret life. My presence, I suppose, stood for the joining of his lives, for I was both private and public.

Charley Bland

I was the new one the women talked about, the first of the season's summer visitors, and they were amused as they always were until there was danger of Charley's conquests turning serious, or lasting too long, so that they were no longer entertaining. So the women hugged me and the men kept their hands on my shoulder long enough for me to feel the warmth of their palms through the brown silk of one of the new dresses my mother was so happy picking out for me as she had done when I was ten.

It was a lovely day in the sun, with the breeze from the river touching shining hair, banked high and sprayed that year. I had been away so long, I had forgotten the easygoing comradeship of people born in the same cradle. I mistook it for happiness. I came into the hall with my mother and father, and my childhood was there to greet me, grown up.

The house was crowded, too, not only with the people I had known before that year, but with glimpses of people who would live with me for so long after it was all over. I couldn't know then that the man I caught a glimpse of that first day would become our ragged angel, Broker Carver. That day he was cleaned up, and with the delicately balanced politeness of a drunk, he came up to my mother and she said, "Anderson, I'm always glad to see you," as if no time had passed between them.

He said, "Who's going to win?" and my mother flirted a little with the person she might have known sometime a long time ago, before Anderson Carver went broke and became Broker, and said, "That would be telling, wouldn't it?" She walked among the men, who begged for the winner, and she kept her reputation intact by refusing to tell.

Broker talked to the women, conscious of their knowledge of him, never presuming, for he was the wreck of a

gallant man. He remembered to flirt with all of them, and
some, the few that I knew would do it and I liked them for
that, teased the shadow of a man who had once been a devil
with the ladies.

He came with Dub Wilson and Sam Cutright, cleaned
up, too, for the day. Dub and Sam stayed close to each other,
as if they were afraid each step would topple them, but,
with their street-corner smiles, pleased to see so many people they had once known.

Later, when the Derby had been run and the people
were beginning to leave, the house that had been Charley's
for one afternoon became his parents' again, and he found
a way to get Broker and Sam and Dub back down into the
town. Plain George "offered them a ride," carted them down
the hill, and came back to get Anne Randolph, who said,
"Charley, you're so sweet," watching their retreating backs.
He looked at her with a pure and silent second of hate. But
by that time Anne Randolph had had her other drink—she
always had two, and she dieted so strictly that two made her
drunk—and she didn't notice that he hadn't answered her.

Broker missed none of these maneuvers, and he would
tease Charley, each year; that, too, as traditional as the Derby.
The first time, a week later, when Charley was taking me to
present me to his friends under the bridge, in much the
same way he had presented me to his family, Broker said,
"Charley got me out of there before I said fuck in front of
the ladies, didn't you, Charley?" And not waiting for Charley
to answer, "That's my swear-to-God high point of the year,"
and then, deriding his own admission, "I take me a bath."

I think it was the presence of Broker that reminded
me of the private, heartfelt capacity for joy in Charley Bland
that seemed so often to have been buffed out of him. On

Derby Day it would come back, burst each spring, as it did each hunting season, a wild plant, a sport, to show that it still lived within him.

That first year the Bland house was more welcoming and noisier than I ever saw it again. The early-May sunlight filled the long living room with the gold light of promise. It was three days before the Kennedy primary, and the women shrieked at each other about where they were driving the candidate, and what they were going to wear and who had had a drink with Jackie, and wasn't she *fab*ulous.

Charley whispered as he passed, "The silk-stocking Democrats are out in force." Daisy told me proudly, "We got sick and tired of the press saying we were a depressed area, so we took every foreign sports car and Brandy's Bentley, even if he is a Republican, up to the airport so we would look better on television. I wouldn't have believed the crowd of hillbillies if I hadn't seen it with my own eyes. Honestly!" "Honestly," that meaningless refrain the women never knew they added, like salt, to their sentences. She drifted away, leaving a possibility, unconscious in me as well as her, of becoming a part of a dream.

I heard Mr. Baseheart, Brandy's father, say to my father, "We don't have anybody else. Rockyfeller's a pinko. To misquote the late lamented s.o.b. Roosevelt, that slimy little Nixon fellow may be a shit but he's our shit."

Daddy was grinning and rolling his julep around in a silver julep cup. He said, "I got no time for California poor whites." Mr. and Mrs. Bland added six julep cups each year for Charley's Christmas present.

Later I heard Brandy, Mr. Baseheart's son, say to someone I didn't know, "He may be a shit, but he's our shit." It was a refrain that year, a counterpoint to the babble that seemed to rise to the ceiling and hover there like balloons of sound.

Mrs. Bland fussed around the room, seeing to things, introducing herself formally to people, and checking to see when it was time to take Dearie upstairs before, as she confided to me later, she upset the apple cart. She said, too, of the people Charley filled the house with, "I never could get quite straight who in this valley was you know and even more difficult who had been you know and wasn't anymore at one of Charley's Derby parties. It's very difficult." She sighed.

Dearie, on the other hand, had a wonderful time every year. Her face got rosier and rosier, until it was red and she began a voyage of indiscriminate love through the room that led to Charley's arm and her exit up the stairs.

It was the one day of the year that Mr. Bland totally approved of Charley. That first day, when I passed close to them, I listened to the two old men, Mr. Bland and Broker, riding up Lacey Creek on their horses grown faster and sleeker with the years, to court the owner's girls and get coal leases up the hollows in the days when people lived at the mine.

Mr. Bland derided mine owners who lived down in the town instead of at the mine, where they could keep an eye on things. They were, he said, as absentee as the Peabody Interests, and he added, looking around the room as if he had not seen it before, that she—Mrs. Bland—had insisted on it. They talked about "old man" Pratt, and the "Eastern interests," and when one of them laughed, telling a story, I heard for the first time the name of Mother Jones.

Mrs. Bland moved, pleased with life, from group to group of the grandchildren and the great-grandchildren of the giants in the earth. Watching her dart among the company, I hear again her telling somebody about the Bland girls, Mr. Bland's close cousins, who were, she said, the be-all and the end-all. The Bland girls of my father's hopes and Mr. Bland's bitterness were, for a minute, ghosts in the room, gliding silently just behind the shoulders of people, shadows of girls in their shadows of white dresses. But she never mentioned Broker's sister Letitia to him. She stayed in a trunk in the attic, and in Mrs. Bland's newer habits.

In that clutched room, I remember gestures and the hints I never looked for, faces in shadow, glimpsed, turned away, glossed with politeness and social smiles for the day. I remember the small eyes of Melinda Cutright, one of Sadie's best friends. She was the older sister of Johnny McKarkle, who had once driven me home from one of the perpetual dances of our growing up, drunk as a lord, and trying to grab at me as he careened his roadster down the hill from the Canona Country Club, the center of the earth in those days for us. I had nearly forgotten him. He was evasive like Charley, another escaper into the dark from the solid citadel on the hill.

Across the room that first Derby party in 1960, I saw Hannah McKarkle, Johnny and Melinda's younger sister. She was wearing a bag dress, worn in New York that year but not yet in Canona. It was the last time I ever saw her. She was then a silly-looking gamine girl, younger-looking than the thirty-year-old I knew she was.

In one brief recall from childhood of her standing like a Nike on the diving board at the Canona Country Club, drunk in a green chiffon dress that billowed in the wind, I saw the ages and changes in gallant Kitty Puss. I saw Haley Potter's face, frozen with old resentment and the clinging snobbery that in our time replaced religion among the "nice" people. Daisy seemed unchanged from when she had played hockey, and was an "honor girl" at camp, and told us all what to do. She had only grown more so, more rigid, more certain; her shadow, Maria, always beside her, had become thin instead of slim. Later, I'm sure it was later on that first day, I caught a glimpse of Tel Leftwich's pre-Raphaelite, sacrificial, blackmailing fury.

They were all there and they are, for me, all there still, passing in and out of the reality and the fictions of my memories, faint and half-formed, recalled as fragments, haunting one of the happiest days of my life, as I go back to that year and that day, when the women were agog over the Kennedy primary and the men were betting on Eddie Arcaro or Bill Hartack or Willie Shoemaker. I heard "Bet the jockey," the echo of Bobby Low, over and over, the conversation and the silences like a litany.

Those were the images, random and accidental, as hard to hold as the patterns in a kaleidoscope, taken into my eyes and kept there in the years of sorrow, surprising when I found them again and didn't know where they came from, surprising now when I conjure up the legends and the glimpses of that first Derby party.

I kept all of them unknowing, as we keep small things on the day of a wedding or a disaster, pictures and shards that would stay with me and become an amalgam of memory, imagination, timeless images in dreams, and betrayed hope that I lived with for so long, after I had gone.

At five o'clock, the magic time, the sun slanted through the French windows and turned their faces younger and sheathed their heads in gold, and the conversations that had raged and fought against the ceiling calmed, lowered, and then went out as everybody waited for "My Old Kentucky Home" to drift from Churchill Downs across the miles to the room we stood in.

Depending on how much bourbon had been drunk and how long the ceremony had gone on with each of them, the new people, and the ones who, as my mother whispered, had been there since the year dot, there were faint and hidden tears, and voices singing, then breaking, then trying to sing again.

Venetian Way won that year, 1960, with Bill Hartack up. My mother said she had warned everybody not to bet on Bally Ache, the favorite, but they wouldn't listen. They never did.

Through the years I stayed there, Venetian Way, Carry Back, Decidedly, ChateauVay, Northern Dancer, Lucky Debonair raced across the television screen and won to the groans of the losers and the shouts of the winners, and my mother saying, "I told you," when she hadn't.

Mr. Bland had died in late January 1966. Mrs. Bland had gone like a sleepwalker through the heavy days of February, so stunned for the first time in a long time by the facts of life that I longed to comfort her, as I had longed to comfort my mother. But they were both women who chose their comforters, and even when she let me come there, she would have no sweetness except from Charley. She would look up from whatever she was doing, or ignoring, or staring at, and say, "I need Charley. Where is Charley?" with the voice of a lost child.

She had bought the new carpet in early April on her return from the Caribbean cruise that she and Dearie decided would do her good. By late April she said she felt well enough and didn't want to be selfish about it, so she set her foot down and stated categorically, she said it that way, that Charley ought to go on with his party. "She said, Your father always enjoyed it so. He would want you to," Charley told me, and his voice had gone so soft about her that I wanted to warn him.

She called Sadie to come back from Kentucky and help her, and since Sadie had never been asked so softly, so sweetly, to do anything, she came, bringing with her a widow who had lingered a little too long just on the young side of aging, and who, at once, became what she had been chosen to be, Charley Bland's newest conquest. He had long since gone back to that form of politeness to strangers. He never mentioned her to me, but my other friends did. They hadn't seen us together for so long that they thought whatever we had managed to keep going all that time was over.

I received the first formal printed invitation ever sent for the Derby party, saying that Charles Bland would be at home on Saturday, May 5. It was sent to my mother's house. My mother took one look at her card and said, "Oh, for God's sake," and threw it in the wastebasket.

In the years that had slipped by, some of Charley's friends had died, some had gone beyond polite drinking into "problems," some had gone rake-thin and were on their obvious way to dying, others had grown fat. Lines that had been hints, then veils over the women's faces, had grown more deeply etched each year.

Broker was surviving them all. We still sat with him at secret times—all our times were secret by then. But when I walked into the house on the fifth of May, there was no Broker, no Dub Wilson, no cousin Sam Cutright, no fat Charlie Estep from the Wayfaring Stranger. Poor Dub had been found in his boardinghouse, dead, and Johnny Mc-

Karkle had died in an automobile accident like so many others who drove too fast around the mountain curves. He had gone over the cliff at Lookout Rock. I could see him still, lingering in air. Hannah's memories and mine have become different fictions. I have always wondered why she wrote about him dying in a drunk tank. I suppose it was because, as I had with Charley Bland, she had had to get him out so often.

Mrs. Bland and Sadie had arranged the new Derby party. They told Charley not to worry about a thing. Mrs. Bland had met an English divorcée on the cruise and she had invited her back for a week. She was one of those English women who get, not fat, but comfortably buxom, and she had a faint Cockney accent left over from leaner years. She had a jolly laugh, and a lilting voice, and large false teeth. Mrs. Bland said she had a "place" in the Bahamas. The woman confided in me, late in the afternoon, when she found out that I "knew" England, that she lived in Stoke Poges. "Near Slough," she said, "but very different. Very beautiful. Full many a flower is born to blush unseen . . ." She forgot the rest and wandered away.

As the mint juleps were passed for the second and third time, she and the widow from Kentucky took to glaring at each other. It made Plain George laugh, and Anne Randolph told him to shut up. Sadie was standing, not with me, but beside me, and she said, "None of this means a damn thing," to herself, but aloud. She sounded surprised and relieved.

It was a changed world. Joy had gone out of it. There was sex, and questing, and too much to drink, and people looking over each other's shoulder as they talked to see who else had been invited. It had become, at last, the kind of party that Sadie and Mrs. Bland understood. Once again

Mrs. Bland had weeded Charley's garden. It was terrible.

I heard Charley's theme song, played on the new record player he had bought for his mother because she said that she missed good music so now that Mr. Bland had gone. I got just as far as the door. Charley and the widow were leaning together, their bodies melting into each other, listening to the Clancy Brothers sing "The Wild Colonial Boy." Charley was nuzzling her fine pink hair and saying, "You found it for me. Oh, I've longed to have it." We had been playing the same record all winter long.

I tried to escape by running up to Charley's bedroom, which had been made into a cloakroom for the ladies for the day. I shut the door and leaned against it. The picture of Jubal and me had been removed from his dresser, and I saw myself and my dog, trapped in the trunk in the attic, growing brown and old and stained. I picked up my coat.

Charley Bland knew my mind as if he had gone to his room with me. When I got to the bottom of the stairs, he was waiting for me. He grabbed my arm hard enough to hurt me, and wouldn't let me go. I don't know why even now. He said, "I can't stand this."

"You don't need me," I said. "You've got the widow, that one or another one. It doesn't matter, does it? Let me go home."

"Oh, God," he whispered. "Not now."

So I stayed. I stayed as I always had when Charley told me to. At five o'clock the men managed to get the level of chatter in the room low enough to hear if not see Kauai King win by five lengths. Nobody sang "My Old Kentucky Home."

I watched Charley, with his arm around the widow again. She had nestled close to him as if she couldn't stay away from bodily contact. His face had a gloss of drink and lust that I had never seen before. It was like the faces of the other men gathered around him, grown older and sunk back into the years that were making them into parodies of their habits and their losses.

As if there were no hatreds, no silence, Charley insisted on taking us all to dinner after everyone had gone. The women sat in a row opposite me on a long banquette in the country-club dining room, the last time I ever went there. So there they are still, the corpulent divorcée from Stoke Poges, not Slough; the widow from Kentucky; Mrs. Bland, littler and stronger than all the others; Sadie, letting her boredom show. Their eyes are dead. They remind me of one of those old photographs of the Dalton gang or the James brothers, staring into space.

Dearie had passed out and been carted off to bed. It was the only continuity in Charley's Derby party, the most positive act of that frozen night.

Charley wouldn't let me go home even then. He insisted on taking me back up the hill for a "nightcap." Mrs. Bland said from the back seat, "Charley, it's time to go to bed. The party's over." He didn't say a word, just kept on driving too fast up the hill. He had drunk himself into a totally sober despair.

They sat in the library listening to the widow's phonograph record, while the sailors sang their way to lift the sails to go to Australia out of Liverpool dock, and McPherson was hanged, and the Irish wars were fought. The songs haunted the night and Mrs. Bland kept saying that they were just lovely. Charley handed the silver julep cups around for the last time; then he motioned me to follow him out onto the terrace.

We leaned against the parapet as I had so many times with Mr. Bland. "I can't stand this anymore." Charley's voice was so quiet with defeat that I had to lean close to hear him, and he pulled his body away as if he had been touched and pawed enough in one evening and couldn't stand a human touch anymore. "I can't stand the pressure. It's killing me. You have something to do. Please go, please please go. Don't you see I'm needed here?"

Then he said, "I'm too old. I'm over fifty years old. It's too late. It's too late for me." He was talking to the trees, as his father had, and letting me hear, in the dark, where the stars were faint above the town and no time passed.

He was crying, the second time I ever heard him cry. I couldn't see his face. It was dark and I was crying, too. Neither of us made a sound.

My julep glass slipped out of my hand, bounced on the stone floor, and rolled away. I leaned down to pick it up and couldn't find it. Above me, Charley said, "Leave it, for God's sake."

I came up from the floor. I stood there, my hand stinging. I had slapped Charley Bland so hard that even in the half-light from the living room I could see the perfect mark of my fingers, dark on his face, before he put his own hand up, too late, to protect himself.

Mrs. Bland called from inside the house, "What are you children doing out there in the dark?"

Ticket to Ride

Hillbilly love songs are the only love songs I know that tell the truth naked, not slant, as Emily Dickinson advises. Slant is for quiet houses, death in bed, and gentle people.

In hillbilly love songs, you leave town from plastic fast-food joints. You say goodbye in front of the Cut Rite drugstore. This death, and it is one, belongs on buses, in two-toned Fords, going down the road feeling bad. Your funeral baked meats are a Moon Pie and a six-pack.

It was cold, though it was getting near to summer again—cold moving from my apartment with a trailer with a Tennessee license, hitched onto the back of a blue-and-white '55 Ford, cold across the town, and cold in the false coziness of my mother's early-American kitchen in the basement where I put back all of the furniture I had borrowed.

Cousin Sam helped me. When we finished, the room looked as virginal as if I had not defiled it, everything in its place again, no ripples, no changes, except the faint nick on the lovely-old-pine-table where Charley had broken a glass by crashing it down in one of his more passionate moments of certainty and promise.

My mother greeted Sam as if he had never been exiled from the hill. She made sandwiches for us to take to the apartment to pack the trailer to go over the mountains. She even found a bottle of beer for Sam in the back of her refrigerator. It had been there for several years. He sat in the car, waiting for me and drinking his beer.

She was cutting bread—she hated sliced bread—when I finally told her what I had done.

"I hit Charley," I said, and I began to cry. "I could have killed him. I wanted to."

"Too bad you didn't, but it's against the law and it's inconvenient." She went on making tuna-fish sandwiches. She wrapped them and put them in a brown paper bag. "The whole thing," she said at last, "was a mistake anyway." With the word "mistake" she closed her book on six years of my life there.

The only true emotion that sustained her through it all was stone Saxon pride. When I had told her I was leaving she said she didn't blame me, that it was about time, and she was, at last, ready to help me, as she had refused to do when, as she said, I was making a damned fool of myself. She had let me go hungry so long as I insisted on living someplace else, and hurting her pride with what she saw was my failure. She had tried to pick up the pieces of her broken plans by telling me that I ought to be "at home" where I belonged. Every widow in her family, she said, had a poorer relation living with them and she saw no reason why I shouldn't do my duty.

But she had given me the money to go to New York and get a job. She backed my buying of the car for five hundred dollars. What visual pride both she and Charley took, she in her Buick, he in his MG, the twin of Kitty Puss's, didn't extend to me. Charley had said, one late night, "You're artistic. You can get away with anything." He spoke from another country.

When we had made the last trip in the Ford, all that was left for me to take across the mountains were my records, my books, some clothes, and the sofa bed that was wide enough to sleep on that my hillbilly neighbor had helped me build for the cabin.

I went through the last motions as you go through the motions of a wedding or a funeral, or any terrible ceremony of innocence, for the others, and for pride. The deepest emotion I saw in anyone was embarrassment. I wonder if when the prodigal left again, as Rilke hints he did, he had to go through the formal dance expected of him. But if he did leave again, it was for different reasons. He was escaping love. I was being exiled from it, or what was left of it: old bottles, old notes found and thrown out when I abandoned the apartment, hints of bright times thrust into the backs of drawers.

I was receiving, at last, the terrible blessing from my harsh country that I had waited for—permission to go, what the song called my ticket to ride. I did not know this then. I know it now.

There was the obligatory cocktail party that Anne Randolph insisted on having, or for once Plain George made her do it; I would never know. I only remember that it seemed less hopeless to go and play at being Tuesday's reason for a party than it would have been to stay away. Being there was its own camouflage.

Because it was late May and the evening was warm, she put the bar on the porch with its high white columns that looked out over the river, the same view as Mr. Bland's, the same river, the same people, but something in it so lost that I remember it as an empty place with nobody there, with something nobody named waiting to happen.

It was a husk of a party, all the joy gone out of it, or maybe it had never been there as I remember them at the beginning. Had seeing them through love, the dancing, the touch, the color, the warmth taken place as a shining beam in my own lonely eye?

There were long pauses in the evening, lacunae of silence and isolation. I stood at the Georgian door of a house that I knew, and didn't know and never would and had been to a hundred times to see a hundred Sunday-afternoon football games, and I listened to the noise from the porch, the litany. I wanted to run, but there were nice people behind me, the kind of people that day after day let the same terrible negation that was happening to me happen all around them, hemming me in with polite murmurs, and I went through the colonial front door with them. They smelled the way Americans do at parties, of scent and baths and shaving soap and clean linen, the cleanest people on earth, and they have no names now nor any sound to them. I no longer mistook their easy hospitality for joy.

I wish there had been furies in the trees, but I was not allowed them. I would have longed for frenzy, for at least the life of nightmare, had there been life enough for longing or frenzy in that dead time when the silence was submerged under babble that seemed so remote. It was not even haunted, that place in the late afternoon in the last of the sun and the breeze from the river. In hell there is no haunting; for haunting there must be regret or hope and there was neither.

Those are the easy horrors. You must see true horror in the filling of a glass, a hand in a pocket easily, the touch of someone's hand on your shoulder by habit easily, the polite smile, the eyes and voice of habit.

There ought to have been some sweetness, some cry, some wind in the branches to lift the women's skirts and knock over the white wrought-iron chairs, skid them across the lawn, grab the limp white tablecloth on the bar and rip it with the bottles to crash onto the soapstone floor.

The doors should have banged in the wind, glass shattered—something, anything to mark the time while I stood there being polite, while Charley leaned on the house wall with Mrs. Bland's divorcée from Stoke Poges not Slough beside him, standing too close, and watching him spaniel-eyed. Obviously she had sneaked past Mrs. Bland's room to his bed. I could see her weighing down the narrow mattress.

The word "love" was used, or I heard it as a whimper, love of objects, love as aesthetic, as habit, as power, as a compliment in the flat evening light: "I just love your dress," "I just love the way she does eggs"; I wanted to giggle at doing an egg.

Passing, they gave me little embarrassed hugs and said, "You have a wonderful time, you hear?" as if I were going to Hilton Head, which somebody across the terrace was saying they just loved.

Hell is not another place. Hell is here—banal, and habitual, with its resident spirit gone away. It didn't even threaten rain. Only rain could have stopped this endless evening, endless chatter, melting ice in endless drinks clutched in their aging genteel little hands.

Daisy, Maria, Haley Potter, Melinda Cutright, all of them went through the same gestures of formal affection they had gone through when I had seen them first six years before. It was easier to do now that Sadie was gone again. The pain for me was shallow, a spur to going. Even defeat had been translated for Anne Randolph into some glamorous promise. "You'll go to New York with all those famous people and just forget about us," she flirted with me.

Kitty Puss said, "Anne Randolph, you never have known when to shut your mouth."

They, who had fed me and then killed that part of me containing warmth and life, were making me go through the last farce, the farewell party, when, from hunger that had gone on for several weeks and that I would not have admitted to a soul, my legs were weak.

I would have been comforted by the truth of the visions of those I had hurt to come there, companions of years that I had forgotten for so long, all the friends from across the world that I had thought, in the blind surge of love, hadn't cared. I wanted one of them to whisper, "For this, these dead, you caused me pain? You walked over my life as they are walking over yours?" The wronged would have been my company, but I had been in this trap for six years and they no longer thought to consider me.

I was finally allowed to leave, and I made those noises of goodbye you make, hardly hearing myself. Plain George walked me to the door, and out into the road. He hugged me and I pulled away for fear of crying. He said, "It's not his fault. You know it's not his fault."

I told him then the only blame I ever cast on Charley Bland. "Yes, yes, it is; but like a fault in marble, a fissure, Charley has a fissure of quartz. It makes a good design." I was laughing as I ran on down the road, and I was glad of that. Plain George called after me the only words of comfort he knew, Bobby Low's parting words so long ago: "You'll be back before you know it."

I walked for the last time down the road where my barn had been and across the hill toward my mother's house. Charley had rented his house to a young couple I didn't know. I could see people inside when I passed; children there, and the plants still veiling whatever strength that room had, if only for me. I kept saying the Lord's Prayer over and over down that dark road, to keep away what threatened to break me.

My mother called good night when I opened the door, as she had when I was growing up, and said, as I knew she would, "Did you have a good time?" and didn't wait for an answer; she never had. "Turn out the lights," and I muttered, "Put out the light, and then put out the light."

Behind me Charley put his hands on my shoulders and we both began to cry. We tiptoed to the basement door. All night we sat in the early-American kitchen. I don't remember that we said anything, but we must have talked to each other, something anyway. I know we sat there until the first light came through the dirty basement windows where my mother's ivy had nearly covered them.

Sometime during that night we made love to each other, angry and wild, on the blue-and-gray hooked rug, rolling halfway under the lovely-old-pine-table that my mother had picked up for almost nothing. It was a flailing, mutual punishment.

I left at nine o'clock in the morning from my mother's coign of vantage on the hill. She was glad to see the Ford and the trailer go—they were as wrong as a pickup truck in front of her pretty house.

When I was finally ready to go that May morning, she thrust two hundred dollars in my hand and said, "Call me if you need any more." She, who had been looked after, in the good years and the bad ones, since she was a child, had no idea that there were any crises that couldn't be faced with two hundred dollars of mad money.

Her last words to me were not what I expected, after all her bitterness. She said, "Don't blame Charley, honey. He's a wounded soldier. It's the first time in his life he almost made it on his own."

I drew the Ford with its trailer from Tennessee into the nice people's parking lot, and the attendant, who I hadn't realized had noticed anything of our lives, came up and leaned his arms on the car in the familiar way of hospitality that hillbillies have and said, "Goddamn, honey, I hate to see this. You don't know how much hope you two give us, all them times of standing up to them people."

To this day I don't know that man's name; in all the years we had been so used to each other, I had never asked. But when it came time to break down the door the others avoided as they would the sorrier parts of death, he knew how to do it.

I was too dead to cry. I met Charley Bland for the last time in a fast-food café near his office, where we sat and stared at the checked oilcloth on the booth table and didn't touch our coffee. It was ten o'clock in the morning. That is one of the facts you remember in disaster or death.

The story always begins, it was ten o'clock, or midnight

or six o'clock, and we were just sitting down to, oh, dinner, breakfast, in a fast-food café with checked tablecloths in the booths. I remember it, the litany goes on, as if it were, or wuz, yesterday, and in those hills it went like this. The telegram come from the army, and the man died, and the car hit, and the world came to an end for somebody. If the somebody is killed or gets out of jail or shoots the sheriff, or the train wrecks or the bus leaves, or the two-toned Ford with the trailer with the Tennessee license, they write a song about it, a true song, as I have tried to write here.

We sat there in the booth with the checked tablecloth and all I could see was Charley Bland's shirt, always clean and white in the morning, his mother saw to that. I could smell the clean cotton of it. I didn't want to look at his face for fear of weakening into tears and I didn't want him to see that. We were not, at that moment, separate. We were being torn apart. I touched his hand and got up and walked the length of the place through an icy world of pink plastic that seemed to go on forever. I left a part of my life on a booth table, like a tip. I remembered to walk straight and not look back. I can still feel my back straighten when I think of it.

My mother had been right. It was like getting out of a battle alive and leaving your buddy wounded in the alien bushes of someplace a dying part of him didn't want to be.

By eleven o'clock I was driving that ridiculous caravan over the first mountains to the east, going through the motions, and even beginning to enjoy them. I have always liked the loneliness of driving. I had no idea then that that going was a blessing, until now when I can tell the story and have the stone drop at last from my heart.

There are other deaths than that of the body, and other exiles than political ones, and they are just as painful, but as Gatsby said, In any case they are only personal. I would wake up afterward for years and think that I was already dead and be surprised at where I was, what country, what bed. I would have been sitting in that timeless moment in the car with the rain and the smell of leather and linen and tobacco smoke, or Charley Bland would have been with me in my sleep.

These dreams were not dramatic; they were not events. In them we simply lived a daily life, even a blessedly boring one, as we would have lived it had that between us not been killed, the killing that had been so slow, that had taken so long and been done with such criminal innocence.

Sometimes I sense that we do live two lives, the one that we have chosen, when we go past the closed doors, the train not taken, the letter not answered. Sometimes we have been led to it, or exiled to it. Then there is the life behind the closed door, the life that comes in dreams of streets that no longer exist, places lived in once, when the walls were yellow brick and the snow never ceased to drift down, and the crows rose when we walked across a never-ending winter cornfield with Jubal and Charley's dog, Birdy, both long dead, checking back.

In these dreams, Charley Bland was younger than he was when I saw him last, as Mrs. Bland and my mother remembered their men. I dreamed him young and joyful, safe and alive in my own soul as he had ceased to be in his.

He was stronger in them than he had been in the other life, the one he lived. He gave me advice I needed; the cool courage that I wanted him to have he had at last, and all through the years until now, in those visitations, I had not realized that he was himself and Bobby Low, too, and my other self within, a guide, my angel.

Our angels have familiar faces, and the faces they assume don't deserve the honor, but deserving has nothing to do with it. Like love, it is not earned. It is grace, if only the grace to be the face and the love in a dream.

They are all dead now, the mothers, the women at the bridge table. Charley, who couldn't wait, took himself out early one morning, after dressing carefully for a day he suddenly couldn't face anymore, in Sadie's glass-fronted modern living room, among the ivies and the *Monstera deliciosa*.

I was sitting on a beach in Turkey and I knew, as you know at the time of a disaster, when we were waiting for the sun to start setting into the Aegean for the night, that he was dead, but not how he was dead. These neural messages are too essential for that. But the message had been right. With the change in time it had been the moment that it happened, in the eastern mountains in a faraway America, lost to me then, at ten o'clock in the morning of a pretty day in May.

He was sixty-four that year, and I was told that he had changed, but the hanged man I saw there, swinging between heaven and earth, was younger than that, as in my dreams, and he wore his houndstooth jacket from Chipp, and his feet in Argyle socks brushed above Sadie's tiled floor, lightly, back and forth in the early morning. He had finally and forever released himself from expectations. It was only his final act. I had seen the unborn man within him die, little by little, for so long.

As Charley Bland changed in dreams—the sleeping

ones and the waking ones that are what we call the stuff of stories—so the others come back in their disguises, none of them whole, a gesture here, a passing event there, a glimpse of a face, some remembered the way they wanted to be, some the way they feared being, some as only I saw them, a shard of a life I didn't know I was noticing at the time. I have tried to bring them alive to tell this story, which they have demanded all this time. After all, as my mother said, Charley was a wounded soldier; he almost made it for the first time in his life.

The houses on the two coigns of vantage over the town have changed and become the homes of other people in other times. Mrs. Bland's house, I hear, or I dream, is full of children and the quietness is destroyed, the decorum smashed, and they run from room to new room. The new people—this is one of the towns where you have to be in a house for at least fifty years to lose the title of new people— have closed in the terrace with glass, so that the children can play and the dogs can romp, and the library has been turned into a television room with a long couch, not the upright sofa of those years.

The colors have changed, I'm told, and all of that beige politeness has been covered with colors that let light and life and brightness into the rooms, which are changed, too. The wall between the formal dining room and the living room has been taken down, and the living room is huge now, and new-looking, and full of furniture that Mrs. Bland would have said was not real.

But when the children have gone to bed and the house is quiet again, on those nights when I have dreamed so strongly of the room in the days when I knew it, I wonder, when whoever lives there and has stayed late at night in the magic corner where the comfortable chair is, reading, or half asleep, if something, a faint noise in the wall, a branch scratching the window, makes them wake up. I wonder if they see, or don't see, or imagine they see, or glimpse and refuse to see, a shadow door open in a wall that is no longer there, and shadow figures pass through it to a dining room that no longer exists, in the half dark of midnight.

Maybe that is what haunting is, the shadows of desire and love and fear left unfulfilled for too long, lodged there until they are exorcised by death, the death of the dreamer, or by a story told. Maybe with the end of this story the unknown people will no longer be haunted and can forget at last that we ever existed.

In my mother's house there are no ghosts but hers; her pride and her courage keep the walls up for whoever is there, the little snort with which she disapproved of things aesthetic or what she called pushy can be heard when a decision is made, a room is changed, a wall is taken down or put up, or they have decided to paint over the wallpaper she bought in Williamsburg.

I'm sure I would have heard it, her little arrogant sniff, and known who it was, but the young people living there, too, with children, think it is their oldest boy, who has a perpetually stopped-up nose, say, "Stop that," and he says, "Honest, it wasn't me."

All she has left is a sniff, for the house was hers entirely. With all her wit and her pride, she never let anything but dreams, first of her father and then of her husband, close enough to haunt it.

You do come alive again after disasters; it takes a long time, and must be secret, lest the others grow impatient. When you do, at last, you have crossed the one more river.

Like in the legends of reincarnation, you are a different person, but sometimes you carry memories of another person, as I have, another life, another childhood, another lost hope that you can't let go until one day permission comes, in a dream, in a story, as it has come to me, and I can leave at last and say goodbye without malice.

But the profane love I bore as my burden has left its residue like a pebble in my hand, shaped by an unknown sea. It has shown me what it is to love, and has become in time a hope without illusion, the recognition of a light glimpsed through the glass, darkly, which is all that we were ever promised.